I'LL BE SEEING YOU
A BRIARWOOD SANITORIUM NOVELLA

SYBIL KNIGHT

Holiday Cover Designer: 3 Crows Author Services
Discreet Cover Designer: Dazed Designs
Editing: Kat Pagan, Pagan Proofreading
Formatting: Dahlia Reign LLC

SOCIALS:

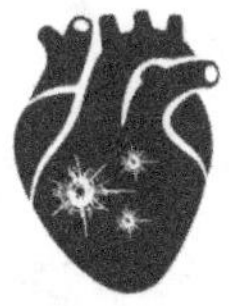

EMAIL: AUTHORSYBILKNIGHT@GMAIL.COM

NEWSLETTER: WWW.SENDFOX.COM/DAHLIAANDSYBIL

FACEBOOK GROUP:
WWW.FACEBOOK.COM/GROUPS/DAHLIAANDSYBILSLITTEDEVILS

INSTAGRAM: WWW.INSTRAGRAM.COM/AUTHOR.SYBIL.KNIGHT

FACEBOOK PAGE: WWW.FACEBOOK.COM/AUTHORSYBILKNIGHT

TIKTOK: WWW.TIKTOK.COM/@QUEENSOFCHAOSBOOKS

AMAZON: HTTPS://WWW.AMAZON.COM/STORES/SYBIL-KNIGHT/AUTHOR/B09QW5R3MB

DEDICATION:

*T*O EVERYONE WHO SAID YOU CAN'T PUT *THAT* ON THE FIRST
PAGE OF A *C*HRISTMAS NOVELLA,
WATCH ME...

(*A*LSO, *L*ARISSA, TELL YOUR HUBBY THAT MARRIAGE IS UNTIL
DEATH. BUT OUR TRAUMA BOND IS *FOREVER.*)

TRIGGER WARNING:

Please be advised that the male lead in this book displays sociopathic tendencies. And the relationship portrayed between him and the female love interest should in no way reflect how anyone should be treated.

If you come across someone like this in the real world, the author urges that you check the locks on all your doors and windows.

But between these pages, in the land of fiction, there's no point in trying. Because he's already inside the house...

That said, the author asks that you heed the following list of potential triggers:

- Overall sexually explicit and violent content
- Accidental (maybe not so accidental) necro
- Death and murder

- PTSD AND TRAUMA
- GRAPHIC INJURIES
- SELF-HARM
- PRESCRIPTION DRUG USE/ ABUSE
- MENTIONS OF PAST CA AND CSA (TO MC/S NOT BY)
- STALKING/ B&E
- SUICIDAL THOUGHTS/ ATTEMPTS
- SOMNO
- MEDICAL GORE/ ABUSE
- VOYEURISM
- MENTAL HEALTH REP
- NONCON/DUBCON/CNC
- COERCION AND MANIPULATION
- FORCED INCEST (TO MC/S NOT BY)
- MENTIONS OF ALCOHOL & ILLICIT DRUG USE/ ABUSE
- DOLLIFICATION
- USE OF A SEX DOLL
- SEXUAL DYSFUNCTION
- FORCED DRUGGING
- MASKED ASSAILANT
- BLOOD PLAY/ PERIOD PLAY
- AND MORE...

HAVE YOU READ THE TRIGGER WARNING?

IF NOT, THERE'S TIME TO FLIP BACK.

STILL GOING?

OKAY, BUT PLEASE DON'T SAY I DIDN'T WARN YOU.

BLURB:

Even serial killers have a type. Unfortunately, tonight, that type is you.

You can feel it, can't you? The way I've been watching you night after night. Patiently waiting for you to turn around and give me a glimpse of those eyes.

Don't be shy. I know you want this as much as I do.

Atta girl. Look at you! You're perfect. Just fucking perfect. Like I knew you would be.

The more that I think about it, you could be her twin.

You know what that means, right? You're the one. At the very least, the *next* one. Maybe the *last* one if you don't fuck this up like all the others.

We can figure that out later, though. When I move on from watching to doing.

Because you might not see me, sweetheart. But I'll be seeing you. Real soon.

I'll Be Seeing You is a dark standalone novella and a spin-off of The Renegades Series. The focus is dark romance so please heed the trigger warnings at the beginning of every book.

(PS: For anyone wondering if that doctor with all the tattoos was real or a figment of Marisela's imagination, you're about to find out…)

PROLOGUE
HIM

Guess I was wrong.

She wasn't the one for me. Bitch screamed and forced me to slit her throat before I was two thrusts deep.

Would I have killed her anyway? Of course. She'd ripped off my mask and seen my face. But at the very least, I preferred that my pussy stay warmer a bit longer. Tighter too. Everything loosened up after they stopped breathing. After the blood stopped pumping. Till rigor kicked in but then so did the smell. Not rot. That took a day or two. But the odor of death. Something imperceptible to most but clung to the inside of my nose like tobacco. Worse than that was when they pissed themselves, though.

That was not my kink. I didn't like fucking 'em dead. I liked the stillness. The quiet. The submission. The wide eyes that looked into my soul and realized I didn't have one.

Maybe I never did. Wasn't sure if souls were hereditary. If so, I was fucked from the get-go.

The mattress squeaked with the back-and-forth motions of my thrusts. Enough to have the headboard tapping against the wall but not so much that the neighbors would think my girl here was having anything more than a good time.

I grabbed the top of her head, now limp and hanging on by a sliver of meat and muscle, and forced her to look at me. Eyes so blue I could drown in 'em. Drink 'em down.

She had eyes just like these. Except she'd never look at me. Just stare past me. Like I didn't exist. Like she wasn't doing shit no mother should be doing to a kid.

I was fucked. But that woman was a fucking monster. And I couldn't get her out of my head. No matter how many times I killed her.

That's right. She'd been my first. Carved a set of matching red bracelets into her wrists and watched the tub water turn pink. When I was eight.

It was all in my chart.

What wasn't in my chart was why. Because no one mentioned that. No one cared what turned a poor kid from the trailer park into a cold-blooded killer.

Don't get me wrong; they'd pretended to care. They sure as shit ran all the right tests, put my brain under a microscope and looked for the defect. They weren't gonna find it. Because there wasn't shit wrong with me then.

Not like there was now...

Fuck, this pussy felt good. I was getting there.

Getting closer to that high. That release I needed. But then my mind wandered back again. To that night. To what she'd done to set me off. I tried to stop it, but my thoughts always went there…

What they should have been asking the whole time was what was wrong with her. The bitch who'd been molesting me since I was old enough to realize it wasn't my diaper she was interested in changing. They claimed you couldn't remember shit that young. I couldn't forget it. Or what she looked like in that tub. Too drunk to lift her arm and stop me from slashing at it. Long brown hair and bright blue eyes.

Those eyes kept me focused. Kept me suspended between the past and the present. Kept my dick hard.

Fuck, fuck, fuck…

I had to hold back my moan as I came all over her stomach. The dead girl bleeding out *all over her* mattress. She sure was pretty, even with the gaping wound circling her throat like a string of rubies from Tiffany's. Or maybe because of it.

Still, *she* wasn't *her*. My mother. No one was. No one could be.

I knew it was cliché. A serial killer with mommy issues. Then again, shit was cliché for a reason. That reason being it made fucking sense.

CHAPTER ONE
HIM

"Good night, Doctor…" Her words trailed off and she smiled. The forced kind that told me she wasn't sure if she recognized me or not. But the rose emblem on the embroidered lab coat *told her* I belonged here. And I did, just not in the way she was thinking.

"Good night, Juliet."

That gave her pause, a light shiver traveling up her spine that had her rocking back on the heels of her orthopedic shoes, before her eyes flicked down to her badge and her lips tipped up with relief.

That wasn't how I knew it. Her name. But she didn't need to know that.

I tugged on the sleeves of my white coat, a nervous tick—I wasn't nervous, more like excited—and pushed off the counter with a bounce in my step. It had been six months since my last kill. And that itch was starting to turn into more of a burning ache. A need. Like breathing took too much effort unless I was popping someone else's pills. That didn't cure the ache, though. Just dulled it enough that I could forget for a few hours.

I'd thought the pretty little thing they kept locked away upstairs would be the solution to my growing problem. Our most recent admission. I'd seen them carry her in, wave after wave of dark hair covering her eyes as they'd brushed past me. So I'd pushed into her room, grabbed her chart, and waited for her to notice me.

My stomach had twisted. They were the wrong color. Green instead of blue. And as much as I'd tried, I couldn't get passed 'em.

But Nurse Keller was just my type. A bit young, more naïve than I liked them. But her eyes were perfect. More ocean than sky blue. With little flecks of gold that danced when she smiled at me.

I tipped my hat at her and watched her *watch me* exit the secure unit with a beep of a keycard. Down the maze of halls and out the front door. The first slap of fresh, cold air always had the bumps rising on my skin. That prickly sensation that came whenever you were getting away with doing something you weren't supposed to be doing.

I fought that urge to peek over a shoulder as my feet kicked up the occasional stone in the driveway, the gravel crunching with each step I took closer and closer to the old beaten-down Wagon I'd stashed at the side of the building a few years back. Solid frame, despite the rust and cracked leather interior. She was no show pony, but baby girl sure did purr when I kicked 'er engine on.

I swallowed down a handful of the white tabs I'd pocketed, Xannies by the looks of 'em, and tapped my hand on the steering wheel, tuning out the humming sound coming from the dash. I hated wasting the gas but it was cold as fuck outside and I had at least another hour before shift change. Then I lifted my arms, using the flats of my palms to brace my head, and leaned back in my seat.

Might as well get comfortable.

CHAPTER TWO
HIM

I woke with a start. My hands digging into the seat's interior to keep the rest of me upright as I cracked my neck. Trying to shake that feeling you got when your brain insisted you were falling but you were sitting perfectly still. *Fuck.*

The time blinked back at me from the center console. 2:00 AM. I'd knocked out for almost three hours.

"Def Xannies," I grunted to myself before shifting into drive and propelling the Wagon out the gates at the end of the twisty road that led to the main building. It was leading away from it right now. The towering silhouette of Briarwood Sanitorium getting smaller and smaller in my rearview while the rose emblem on the lab coat I'd tossed beside me stayed the same size.

I should have known better than to pop so many pills with a long night ahead of me. But the waiting had had me on edge. Had my knee bouncing and all that pent-up energy bubbling over.

I'd done it to myself. Truth was, I didn't need to wait.

I didn't need to follow Nurse Keller home to know where I was going. I'd gotten her address from the employee files. But I enjoyed doing it. I enjoyed watching 'em in their natural habitat for a bit. I enjoyed fantasizing about that first encounter. Imagining how they'd taste. How they'd feel. That moment between life and death. How long I could keep 'em suspended there. Like picking out a lobster from a fish tank before the chef boiled 'em alive.

Except, in this instance, I was both serving up *and* eating my meal.

Thirty minutes later, I was pulling up to a modest little townie. Lower-income with the kind of neighbors who were good at minding their business. It was the only one without a string of Christmas lights and sat nestled between two houses off one of the busier streets. Which had me rounding the block until I found a spot to park. I wasn't worried about a ticket. Shit wasn't registered in my name. That didn't mean I wanted the inconvenience of having my Wagon towed.

By the time I was creeping up the front steps and slipping a hand into the flowerpot where Juliet'd stashed a spare key, the entire house was blacked out. Minus one window, where a stream of light peeked out from underneath the blinds that I knew likely belonged to the only bathroom. The residents on this street weren't keen on remodeling these older buildings and plumbing was fucking expensive.

The front door creaked when I shoved it open, and I held my breath as I crept up the stairs, careful to keep my steps soundless as I glided my feet from one to the next.

Bracing myself on the banister as the scent of her bubble bath got stronger the closer I moved towards the door. I reached out an arm, using the tips of my fingers to slowly guide it forward on its hinges. Pausing in my tracks when the soles of my shoes splashed against the tiled floor and soaked into the carpet on the other side.

I shifted from one foot to another, as my brain tried to keep up with what my body was feeling. And then I looked over. At her. At the tub. At the bubbles cascading over the lip. At the unnatural color of the water. I knew that color. I saw it in my nightmares. In my dreams too.

What. The. Fuck.

CHAPTER THREE
HIM

I rushed forward, my foot catching on a particularly slippery tile and my ass hitting the ground before I jumped up again and scrambled for the tub. I dove my hands inside and fished around, until I was shoulder deep in the bath water and dragging out Juliet's limp body. The past and present twisting into some sort of perverse nightmare as I wrapped a towel around each of her wrists and secured 'em with hair ties she'd left out on the bathroom counter. Then I carried her down the hall and placed her on the bed.

The cuts were diagonal, which meant she'd been serious. This wasn't some shit she was doing for attention. Not home alone. Not in the middle of the night when no one was supposed to be watching.

I paced back and forth across the little ten-by-ten room, tugging the mask I'd fashioned from an old CPR dummy off my face and running a hand over my shaved head. I could still smell the fresh layer of white paint I sprayed across the front, feel the slightly jagged edges I hadn't had time to file all the way down after I couldn't get the blood off my old one, as I glanced over at Nurse Keller.

She was breathing. I felt her pulse under my thumb but I couldn't be sure how much longer that would last. I didn't know *how long* she'd been there at the start, how much blood she'd lost.

Fuck! I punched a fist-sized hole into the closest wall. I needed this release. I needed it tonight.

I glanced over to where she was bleeding through the bleach-white towels, her head kinked to one side and her tits on display like a fucked-up offering from some more fucked-up god.

I could... It wasn't like it would be all that hard. I peered down at my zipper. 'Cept I wasn't all that hard either.

Now that was fucking weird.

She was the perfect victim. Lifeless but still alive, quiet, no ugly neck wounds to grapple with. Still, it didn't *feel* right. I hadn't done it. She wasn't looking at me. She'd never even seen me. I could see all of her, though.

I took a tentative step forward, my wet shoes making that sloshing sound against the carpet as I eyed her from tit to toe. From wide hips to bare pussy. She didn't look like the type of girl to shave, but I could appreciate the view it gave me. I dropped to my knees. This time in front of the bed, instead of the wet bathroom floor, and set each one of her thighs on a shoulder.

It had been a while since I'd tasted a woman like this. Never really saw the point unless I was getting something in return. And I didn't mean fucking head. I meant information, a stash of pills, an *extra badge and keycard.*

But seeing as nothing about tonight was the norm, I leaned forward, took a deep breath, and swiped my tongue over her cunt. Enjoying the silence, the nothingness as I did it again. And again. Not stopping until the similar odor of old pennies replaced the scent of soap and pussy juice. Reminding me that the girl sprawled across the bed, the girl whose bodily fluids were smearing across my face, was also bleeding out.

CHAPTER FOUR
HIM

I pushed to my feet and tugged Juliet higher up on the bed. Propping her shoulders on some of those million decorative pillows women seemed to hoard for no particular reason. Watching her arm slide off, only to be forced to grab a flatter frillier one to keep her wrists elevated and level with her heart.

Never understood the point of owning something you had no intention of ever using. Then again, guess I was *using* these ones now to help reduce the bleeding. Nurse Keller had over a dozen in this bedroom. Me? I had precisely two pillows to my name, and that was because I'd clipped the second of 'em back when they thought it was smart for me to have a roommate.

That experiment didn't last long. Poor fucker had hung himself from the only loose tile in the ceiling within a week. 'Least that was what the paperwork would tell ya.

I wouldn't tell ya shit. I wasn't a snitch.

I yanked my shirt over my head and stripped out of

the rest of my wet clothes. Walking around bare-assed in Juliet's house wasn't the most gentlemanly thing to do, but I'd been here to kill her. It wasn't like manners were something that mattered in this situation. Besides, I didn't want to ruin the only clean outfit I'd brought with me.

Might need it later. Once I figured out what the fuck I was doing here.

I snooped around various drawers and cabinets and found a shit-ton of nothing. Nurses were supposed to keep emergency kits on hand, weren't they? Seemed like the medically sound thing to do. Though I was pretty sure the medically sound thing to do was not slit your fucking wrists in the first place.

I slammed the closet door shut and stomped to the backpack I dropped by the entrance on my way in, digging through the contents until I found the needle and fishing line I kept on me ever since the time my hand slipped on the blade and I nearly severed a fucking finger. Then, using the flame from the stove, I placed the sewing needle I'd swiped off one of the orderlies directly over the flame and waited for the metal to change color before trekking my way back up the steps.

Juliet hadn't moved. You could barely make out the rise and fall of her chest, but my pillow princess was still breathing. What she really needed was some fluids, maybe a blood transfusion. Neither of which was happening here, and I wasn't about to take her out there.

Raking a hand through the mop of hair that didn't exist no more, I stomped forward and began the task of piecing Nurse Keller back together like some homemade stuffed doll. Lucky for her, the gashes weren't as deep as they looked in the tub. But they sure as shit were deep enough to kill her if I left 'em wide open.

Shit wasn't pretty, and it was hard to tie a decent knot with all the blood seeping out. But a few quick flicks of my wrist later and Juliet was good as new.

I craned my neck to eye the zigzag pattern I'd stitched across her wrists. Okay, maybe not as good as new. But at least she wasn't bleeding out all over the goddamn sheets anymore.

CHAPTER FIVE
HIM

Christmas had always been my favorite holiday. We weren't religious or nothing. It was just the only time it was acceptable for my mother to be as drunk as she was every other day of the year—Christmas and St. Paddy's Day too, I suppose. But no one was giving out four-leaf clovers or whatever green shit was on brand on St. Paddy's Day. No one cared if you went hungry on St. Paddy's Day. But Christmas was when the church folks would stop by with canned goods and regifted presents—as well as lots of stares, a shit-ton of judgment, and the occasional Bible.

Was I a little too old for the toddler toys and used coloring books? And were most of those cans expired and bullshit no one in their right mind actually ate? Like creamed corn and some sort of unrecognizable bean? Yup and yup and yup. But at least they were mine. And not much was mine in that trailer.

Something else my ma liked to remind me of whenever she got the chance. Everything I owned was because of her. Including the cock between my legs. Everything except for those toys and coloring books. She was usually too whacked out of her mind to remember me opening them on Christmas morning, when she even bothered coming home, so it was much easier for me to hide everything in the back of the closet without her finding it and trying to hock it at some pawn shop or cash for gold store.

Which was why boredom had me once again snooping around Nurse Keller's townie. This time, for something more festive than the gray-on-gray décor she had sprinkled around the living room with pops of frilly pinks. I spent a good hour or two rummaging through the house before finding a box of old decorations in the attic. Brand-new, still in the packaging but boxed up anyway. I pulled them down, dropped them into the living room, and then began the task of spreading a little holiday cheer...

The interior was all so... dark *and* pastel, if that was a thing? What it really needed was some red and green, some cheesy-ass holiday music, and some baked goods. My stomach grumbled at the thought. I was a sucker for sweets. Probably because those were a rarity too.

So I made my way into the kitchen next, grabbed a half-empty packet of stale crackers from Jules's pantry, and shoved a handful into my mouth as I headed back towards the living room. Where I threw some cheap garland up on the fireplace and a few of those decorative red and green balls into a dish on the coffee table before moving on to the dismantled tree. The box was sealed and there was plastic wrapped around each of the branches. Like the stuff had gone straight from the register to the attic without ever making a pit stop in the house. But at least I had all the pieces to work with.

It took about twenty minutes or so for me to have the damn thing standing slightly crooked on its own, without bothering to read the instructions, its branches properly fluffed and a few string lights strung haphazardly around the middle. Wasn't the best looking tree I'd ever seen but wasn't the worst either.

Then I took my ass back upstairs to the bedroom where my little rag doll was still propped up on the bed. I shoved her to one side, plopped down beside her on the mattress, and flicked on the tv.

CHAPTER SIX
HIM

I flipped through channel after channel before settling on some black-and-white Christmas movie I remembered watching as a kid. The one where the chump on the screen takes all the good shit in his life for granted and thanks to a "holiday miracle" gets a second chance to do that shit over.

Like I said, I didn't believe in that kind of stuff. Do-overs. Fixing shit that certainly wasn't fixable. Angels getting their wings. *God.*

I mean, what kind of god gave kids to people who certainly didn't deserve 'em?

What I did believe in was that life was fucked. Especially for guys like me. And I guess chicks like Nurse Keller here. Didn't know what was so bad that the woman thought her only way out was to off herself, but I imagined it had something to do with all the books I'd found hidden behind a stack of shoes in the closet. Books on childhood trauma and how to move on from it.

Or maybe that was just what I wanted to think, so I

wasn't alone with that shit. My shit. The shit that wasn't fixable.

Without realizing what I was doing, I set the remote down on the nightstand and glanced over at the motionless figure next to me on the bed. She looked like she was sleeping. My good sense and I both knew that she wasn't. She wasn't dead neither though. Just unconscious. While her body decided if it wanted to mend itself or not and mine wondered what she felt like. What it would feel like. To play around with her pert nipples. To touch her. Fuck her.

Couldn't fucking tell ya why now, all of a sudden, my cock was giving me the green light to find out. But fucker was at full mast as I climbed over Juliet's frame, prying her thighs apart with a knee and pressing myself between them.

She was pale. But not deathly. *Not dead,* I repeated to myself.

And then I was trailing a finger over her pussy lips, pushing it inside and shuddering when I noticed how warm she was. Not dry, not cold, *not dead.* I quickly replaced that finger with my cock, inching forward until my balls were pressing against the skin of her ass, before I started rocking back and forth. Her tits bouncing in front of me as I moved slow enough to keep her arms from flopping down but fast enough to get myself off.

I got there quicker than I thought I would too. Thrusting in and out a handful of times before my cum was spilling all over her stomach. There was nothing I wanted more than to come inside her. But I was pretty sure you could knock up an unconscious woman, not a dead one. And as off script as everything was going at the moment, I didn't want my DNA left in either.

Sorry, Georgie Boy, this was no one's wonderful life. No not-so-immaculate conception. Because in the real world, no one got second chances.

Then again, some people never got chances to begin with. First or otherwise.

CHAPTER SEVEN
HIM

"*Look at you, boy.*" The familiar voice hissed in my direction. "*Awfully cozy, aren't ya?*"

I dropped my cock and grabbed for the remote, increasing the volume on the tv while keeping my eyes glued to the screen as I twisted back around on the bed. I knew it was only a matter of time before she popped up—that didn't mean I had to acknowledge her. I shoved a handful of pills into my mouth and washed 'em down with the glass of milk I'd left out on Jules's nightstand. It was slightly sour but I refused to let that shit go to waste.

Growing up broke had this way of settling into your bones, even when you had cash on hand.

"Waste not, want not, right, ma?" Fuck, I didn't mean to say that aloud. Too late. Now there was no chance the bitch was going away. Not when she enjoyed fucking with my head so much.

"*Turn it off.*"

I swatted out a hand. Nothing was there but it was

habit. Like trying to swat a gnat that wouldn't stop buzzing in your ear even when you knew it was gonna be back a few seconds later.

"Turn it off. Turn it off. Turn it off." Now she was chanting it over and over again. I could only assume she meant the tv. The woman hated anything that brought me joy. She also hated anything that took my attention away from her nagging.

I could only imagine what she thought of Jules then.

I glanced down at the nurse in question before squeezing my eyes shut and cupping my hands over the sides of my head. It wouldn't take long for the pills to kick in. Not that they got rid of her completely, just that they made her a little more fuzzy. Her voice a little less clear. Easier to ignore.

I wasn't crazy but that didn't mean I didn't hear things on occasion. Auditory hallucinations, PTSD, fucked-up bullshit with a label... Whatever you wanted to call it, it followed me. Worse than the Ghost of Christmas Past following that Scrooge guy.

But unlike the sound of their screams, unlike all those women I'd butchered over the years, I couldn't kill 'em. Drown 'em out. Chop 'em up and bury 'em.

You couldn't kill things that were already dead. Even if that did little to stop me from trying.

Never told the docs that I was hearing shit, but it didn't take them long to figure it out when they caught me talking to myself. That was when the treatments started, the pills, the therapies that left her taunting me more and louder. None of them cared about curing me. They cared about cutting my brain open.

They wanted to know when the voices started. If they were trauma-induced or just didn't have the chance to develop until puberty. They wanted to know if that's what caused me to slice so deep her hands were almost falling off.

It wasn't. Because there weren't any voices. Just one. Just hers. And she didn't show up until long after I'd killed her...

I pushed myself up off the bed and made my way to the shower, stepping over the puddles of blood and bathwater still covering the tile floor. Then I slammed the door shut and turned the faucet on the hottest setting. Like if I burned my skin off, I could somehow burn her touch away too.

It didn't work. It never worked. But the sound of the shower spray pelting against the glass did help to drown out the whispers until the meds did what they were supposed to do and drowned out the memories too.

CHAPTER EIGHT
HIM

"*Turn it off...*"

I paused what I was doing, the damp washcloth covered in my cum hovering above Juliet's stomach, before I decided to ignore it and continued wiping at her skin. Scooping up the mess I'd made while enjoying the streaks of creamy white mixing with the blood red until the two colors were swirling together like a morbid version of a candy cane.

I smelled like her soap now and she smelled like me. Fucked up, sure. But no one could claim I wasn't fucking festive. She almost looked as good as the Christmas decorations I'd spread out around her living room. I grinned, dropping my mouth into a frown when it started up again.

"*Turn it off...*"

I squeezed my eyes shut, tighter than before, clamping my jaw—teeth against teeth—until all I could hear was the blood rushing in my ears, the humming in my temples instead.

"Turn it off..." The voice was louder this time, softer, sweeter too. As sweet as the honey my ma used to mix into the cold meds before she forced me to choke 'em down so she could...

I shook my head, tossing the washcloth onto the floor, and stuffed a finger into each ear. "Shut up, shut up, shut up," I grunted over and over until I was screaming it. "Shut up! Just shut the fuck up!"

"Okay," she replied, which had me peering up from between Juliet's legs. Then flying off the bed, my dick wet and flopping against my thigh as I backed myself against the closest wall.

She never did that. She never agreed. Never stopped. Never said okay.

"I'm sorry..." And she sure as fuck never apologized. *"But can you please turn it off..."*

I glanced over to where some Hallmark movie had started playing on the screen, my glare bouncing to the remote on the nightstand and back. Then I carefully closed the distance, powered down the tv, and waited.

Silence, followed by a sigh and a mumbled, "Thank you."

Yeah, fuck that.

I snatched my shit off the ground, stuffed my feet into my damp shoes, and tucked the washcloth into my pocket—I was in a hurry but I wasn't fucking stupid—before making a beeline for the door. I'd just wrapped a hand around the knob when...

"Don't leave me. Please," she whispered, and my feet froze to the spot. My clothes tumbling out of my arms as I turned on a squeaky heel and found Juliet awake. Blue

eyes staring at me. Seeing me for the first time even if it wasn't the first time.

"What did you say?" I asked her.

"I said... please don't leave..." she answered me. I didn't know if it was real. If *she* was real or if I'd just graduated to the part where I was seeing shit too now.

"Okay," I told her anyway, waiting until she'd rolled over onto her side before climbing into bed beside her.

She didn't say anything else after that.

CHAPTER NINE
HIM

"Stop fucking squirming," I grunted, my eyes still squeezed shut as I tugged on the covers and flipped over onto my other side, dragging more than half the blanket with me. The soft, fluffy blanket.

"Sorry," a voice mumbled back, and I shot upright on the bed. I'd almost forgotten I wasn't alone *and* that my mask was still on the nightstand where I'd left it.

I reached out an arm, snatched it up, and shoved it over my head. I looked fucking ridiculous: bare-assed, covered in tattoos, with nothing on but a white piece of hollowed-out plastic strapped to my face. But here we were. Glued at the hip, in some *Twilight Zone* episode of the *Odd Couple* where my face would give me away but my cock wouldn't.

It shouldn't have mattered, considering she'd seen it last night. (Both my face and my cock.) Either way, I had to kill her. I was going to kill her. Just felt like a waste after all that effort I'd put in to saving her. Like flipping a puzzle off the kitchen table the moment you were done putting it together.

I stretched out my sore limbs until each of my shoulders made that popping sound, and then stood from the bed with a groan. I was already fucked. I'd been due back on the unit hours ago. Might as well be fucked and fed.

"What d'ya want for breakfast?" I called out from the door, one hand braced on the frame. I didn't bother turning around. *My ass was up for grabs too, I guess.*

"I'm not hungry. Thank you," she replied.

"I didn't ask if you were fucking hungry, Jules."

"Jules?" she parroted.

"Yeah, those eyes of yours look like sapphires. Besides, Juliet seems too formal for the guy who saved your fucking life."

She was crying into her pillow. Trying to hide it but I could hear her. "I wanted to die, though," she whispered.

"And I wanted to be the one to kill ya," I muttered to myself. "Can't all get what we want, now can we?"

Obviously, she could hear me just as clearly. And *that* had her full-on sobbing. Which didn't make sense to fucking me. If she wanted to die so goddamn bad, what did it matter who was the one doing it? I mean, it mattered to me. It was kinda my thing, but why the fuck should it matter to her?

This was exactly why I liked my women quiet. They were a lot easier to deal with when they weren't talking. When they *couldn't* talk.

I counted to five in my head, like all the quacks taught me to do—*shit didn't work, by the way.* Not when it came to my "homicidal urges" but the brief pause did keep me from yelling at her again.

"I'm making eggs. Tell me how you prefer 'em done or you're getting 'em how *I* prefer 'em done."

"Scrambled..." she said, and it took everything in my power to not say *thank fuck.* Trying not to kill someone was worse than pulling teeth, and I'd pulled out plenty of those.

"What else?"

"Thank you?" she said it like it was a question, and I dragged a hand down my face.

"No, Jules. I mean, anything else to eat... or drink. You want coffee or something?" I heard a rustling of the sheets and spun back around to find her trying to swing herself off the bed. "What the fuck are you doing?"

She froze. Her wide eyes dropping to my limp cock, traveling up the lines and grooves of my abs—probably hitching on the occasional tattoo—before landing on the plastic covering my face. "I, ah, I have to go to the store. I didn't buy more coffee 'cause, well, you know. And I'm almost out of juice."

I shot out an arm, gesturing to the bed. "Keep your ass right there and give me your phone." She looked like she was trying to decide if she wanted to question me, and we sure as fuck didn't have all morning for her to get the courage to do that, so I added, "I'm guessing you got one of those delivery apps. We'll order you some groceries."

CHAPTER TEN
HER

My heart stopped the moment I stepped foot in the living room. Actually, I hated when people said that. It wasn't medically accurate. My heart didn't stop. It would have been easier if it did. Instead, it skipped a beat. An irregular palpitation that had me feeling like I was both dying and painfully alive as my eyes swept across the fireplace, the coffee table, the movie playing on the tv screen, finally landing on the tiny tree in the corner. The ornaments and the festive knickknacks...

I recognized everything. Every bow, piece of tinsel and garland. I knew where they came from. Just not how they got here. In this room. In front of me. Natalie had bought it all and dropped it off a few months back. A house warming present she said. I had to focus on my breathing to keep from shoving her out the door so I could get the bags out of my sight. But I did good. I waited until she was walking back down the steps to her car before rushing upstairs and tucking everything away in the attic. And then I did my best to forget about them. To pretend those boxes weren't there. But now they were all here again. Out in the open.

Twinkling and glowing and flickering at me.

I closed my eyes and blinked a few times but none of it would go away. No matter how much I tried. No matter how much I imagined it all packing itself up and stowing itself back in the farthest corner of the attic.

But when my lashes fluttered open again, I realized my feet were moving. I didn't remember them doing it. Or how my arms started tearing at the glass ornaments. Ripping them down and sending them flying across the room. I could hear them shatter, though. I could hear the thud of furniture tipping over. The sound of heavy boots stomping my way and the feel of someone's arms wrapping around me, squeezing tight, pulling me back. And then all the screaming that followed.

It was coming from me too. I knew it was. My throat was on fire, my face hot to the touch, my jaw aching. But I couldn't stop myself.

"Calm the fuck down!" a deep voice grunted from behind me. Close enough to my ear that I could feel the warmth of his breath even through his Annie mask.

It wasn't him, though. It wasn't Robbie. It was the man from my bedroom. The man who promised not to leave—and he hadn't. He was still here. He was holding me. Dragging me into the kitchen. Sitting me down in the chair and grabbing a broom and a dustpan. And then he was cleaning up my mess.

He was still cleaning it up when the groceries arrived. It didn't stop him from answering the door in nothing but a bathrobe or me from watching the way the muscles in his arms flexed when he rolled up the sleeves and dumped everything out on the counter before splitting it between the cupboards and the empty pantry shelves.

I continued to watch him as he began cracking eggs into the hot pan, humming to himself as he added cheese and salsa next.

CHAPTER ELEVEN
HIM

"Eat." I dropped the plate in front of Jules on the table. It landed with a clatter. But she didn't move to touch it. "It's not fucking poisoned. If that's what you're thinking," I told her. "I'm more of a *hands-on* kinda guy."

I laughed. She didn't. Which meant Nurse Keller here didn't have a sense of humor because that shit was fucking funny.

I rolled my eyes, nearly popping a blood vessel as I forced the edge out of my tone. "Just do me a favor and fucking eat it... *please.*"

Yeah, that last one was fucking hard. But this girl used manners like a crutch. Might as well toss 'em back at her and see if they stick.

She slid the plate closer to her chest and started picking at her eggs with a fork. I plopped down across from her, yanking the oversized fluffy pink robe tighter across my chest. Oversized to her. The thing barely fit me.

And I know what you're thinking. Did I answer the door for the delivery guy like this?

Sure did. On the off chance my disappearance made the news—*it wouldn't if Burke and Hare had anything to say about it and they did*—I had to do my best to stay covered up. At least for everyone I wasn't planning on killing.

"I was gonna call you out of work," I said, breaking the silence as I shoved another forkful of eggs into my mouth. Manners were her thing, not mine. "But looks like you beat me to it." I lifted a questioning brow, only to realize she couldn't see it.

Juliet shrugged, taking in more air than food and pretending to chew both. "Didn't want them to have to find a replacement at the last minute."

"Suicidal *and* considerate." I chuckled. "Be still my heart."

Her lip twitched and so did my cock. Some fucked-up part of me actually liked making her smile. Who would have thought? Not me, that was for goddamn sure.

"So, why'd ya do it?" I asked, and she jerked back like I'd slapped her. Maybe I should have approached the topic a little more gently, but seeing as I'd broken into her house last night to murder and fuck her, not necessarily in that order even if it usually worked out that way, I figured we were beyond discussing the weather.

"Why does anyone do anything?" Another shrug.

"Well..." I leaned forward, shoving my plate onto the floor and listening to it shatter. She was pissing me off and I wanted to startle her. To make sure she was paying attention. I didn't ask shit because I was interested in idle chitchat. I asked because I wanted to fucking know. "Take me for instance, I break into women's houses and slit their throats 'cause mommy liked to touch me when I was sleeping…" I glanced down at my bloodied knuckles and flexed a finger, one at a time, until pain was radiating up my wrist. "…and when I was awake and when she was bored or horny or couldn't get a fix…"

I flattened out my palm and slammed it down on the table between us. Juliet jumped and I leaned back again.

"Now you know my secret. So tell me yours. Who touched ya, Jules?"

CHAPTER TWELVE
HER

I couldn't explain what it felt like. But maybe that was the problem... the fact that it didn't feel like anything. It was just going through the motions. Smiling because it was what you were supposed to do and eating because it was what you were supposed to do. Going to work and coming home because it was what you were supposed to do.

The worst part was thinking that if you did everything you were *supposed to do*, that maybe you'd finally feel how you were supposed to feel. Maybe you'd feel like everyone else. Maybe you'd... just *feel*. In general. At all.

But the only thing I could feel were the tears trailing down my cheeks. I wasn't sad. These weren't sad tears. I wish I was sad. I wish I could be sad. Being sad meant that you knew what it meant to be happy, and I didn't know much about either.

I wiped at the snot bubbling under my nose—I couldn't imagine what my stepmother would think if she saw me looking such a mess—only to have my hand slapped away and replaced by a piece of rolled-up paper towel.

"Will you stop fucking crying already," he grunted, the sound muffled by the mask that didn't make sense for him to wear anymore. Not if he really was here to kill me. And something told me that he was. That something being *the man himself.* More than once.

And even if he wasn't, a mask couldn't hide what parts of him I'd recognized. I mean, not *those* parts. I wasn't looking at those parts. I was just dizzy from all the blood loss.

I meant his stature. Guys that tall with shoulders that wide didn't exactly blend into the crowd, especially at Briarwood. The other physicians were on the opposite end of the BMI chart. More lean meat than actual muscle, except for Dr. Burke, whose physique would have made for a nice Sunday roast.

I glanced down at the job my would-be murderer had done on my arms. The odd crisscross pattern, unlike anything I'd ever seen before, was much more kindergarten art project than med-school graduate. I guess It was safe to assume that, that lab coat was a disguise too. Though I had to admit it looked better on him than the robe he'd yanked off the back of my bedroom door.

He rolled up each of the rose-pink sleeves over his biceps till they were busting at the seams and speared another sliver of runny egg before bringing his fork to his mouth, his jaw clicking when he chewed. I wasn't sure if it was out of annoyance or habit.

"Sorry." My reply was definitely out of habit.

"And stop fucking apologizing," he barked. "Why the fuck are you always apologizing?"

Because it was the best way to avoid an argument.

It was the truth but I kept it to myself. Like most things. People didn't want the truth. They didn't want to hear that you were drowning, barely keeping your head above water. No, they wanted you to say: *I'm great! How are you?* They wanted to talk about themselves and they wanted you to listen. But first, they had to pretend. Pretend they were actually asking. Pretend they cared. They didn't. Just like I didn't care about what kid was winning what award, or who was playing soccer, or how old little such-and-such was turning this year.

I admit it. I pretended too. We all did. But pretending was much easier when you kept things light. Ask how much propranolol you can get away with signing out before the pharmacist starts looking at you funny, and suddenly you find yourself locked on the other side of those unit doors. For me, death seemed much more appetizing than being trapped.

So that was why I did it. I doubted that was the answer he'd been wanting, though. Which was why I didn't answer him at all. It seemed like the safer bet.

"I asked you a question, Jules," he hummed while twirling the tip of a steak knife over the pad of his finger, pressing down hard enough to cause a trickle of blood to drip along the webbing of his hand. It didn't appear to bother him. It didn't bother me either. I wasn't afraid to die. I was afraid of how long it would take for the dying to be over.

"You asked me *a few* questions," I grumbled into my glass of OJ, flinching when I realized I'd said it aloud.

"I did, didn't I? And you haven't answered any of 'em."

"Sor—" He cocked his head to the side. I swallowed down the rest of the word and quickly corrected myself. "What question would you like me to answer first, Mister...?"

"You want my name, *Miss* Keller?" He grinned—I could see the way the mask moved up on his face—and I nodded. "Sure, why the fuck not?" He dropped the knife onto my half-empty plate, scooped them both up, and deposited them into the sink with a loud *clatter*. Then he stepped over the broken pieces on the floor, scraped the leftover food into the garbage disposal, and turned on the faucet. "It's Cain," he said, pausing as the grinding mechanisms rattled the lower cabinets. "Just Cain. No Mister. Got it?"

"Cain?" I repeated. "That's very..." I tried to find the right word. Something that didn't come off too judgy. "...biblical?"

He shrugged a single shoulder while setting the plate into the dishwasher and kicking the door closed again. "Yeah, my ma didn't name me after no good book, Jules. More like her favorite thing in the whole wide world. But calling your newborn *Coke* woulda been a little too *up the nose.*" He tapped a finger to a nostril and made an exaggerated inhalation sound as he slid back into the chair in front of me. "Your turn, sweetheart. Which ona your parents got you all fucked up? I know it's gotta be one of 'em?"

CHAPTER THIRTEEN

HIM

I'd never given any of my girls my name before. Not that they could tell anyone if they wanted to. There just wasn't much time to sit around and swap bedtime stories. Usually.

I glanced towards the window, eyeing the blizzard forming outside. *There was plenty of time now, it seemed. No one was going anywhere with the roads looking like that.*

I grabbed another knife from the butcher block on Jules's counter, dragged my chair across the linoleum while kicking at the ceramic still scattered all over the floor until my leg was pressing against hers, and dropped back down in my seat. She didn't pull away from me as I moved her dark hair out of her face and flipped it over her shoulder. She did sit higher though. Like someone had tugged her spine straight.

"Who hurt you, Jules?" I lowered my mouth to her ear. "Come on, you can tell me. It'll be our little secret." I watched the hair rise on the side of her neck and knew

I'd struck a nerve. It was fucked up. To use the words my ma used to whisper to me before she stopped caring if I told anyone or not. But *I* was fucked up. I also wanted to know the answer and didn't care how I went about getting it.

Nurse Keller leaned her head to one side so she could look at me, her eyes flicking up to meet mine. "My father."

"Not very original. But I'll take it." I slapped a palm on the table, the other one clutching the knife I held at her back. "What he do?"

She shook her head. "I really don't want to talk about—"

"Did I ask if you wanted to do it?" I barked before she could finish speaking. "You know all that shrink stuff. At least you should. If you wanted to talk about it, it wouldn't be a fucking thing. But keep talking about it, and then it doesn't bother you so much."

That last part wasn't as true as everyone liked to tell ya. But a white lie never hurt none. Sometimes it was less painful than the truth.

"I can't..." She stared at me with wide eyes, the kind that little deer had before some hunter clocked his mom in that animated movie.

Disney got a few things right, I guess.

"Ya can. Ya just need a little motivator to want to." I nodded towards the knife in my hand, and she turned in her seat to glance at it.

Then she turned back around to look at me. "Do whatever you have to do."

"Oh, this ain't for you, sweetheart." I slid my arm off

the top rail of her chair and lifted the blade to just under my jaw. Pressing until I could feel the warmth trickle down my throat, the rise and fall of my Adam's apple causing the edge to bite deeper when I spoke. "It's not much of a threat when ya want to die, but ain't nurses supposed to protect and serve? Ain't that in your oath or something?"

She jumped up, grabbed a clean rag from a cabinet, and pressed it to my neck before I had time enough to watch what she was doing. "That's cops, you idiot," she huffed out.

"What is?" I asked, peering up into those blue eyes of hers while she focused on whatever superficial damage I'd done—*I wasn't the one who was suicidal here.*

"Protect and serve, that's their motto. You're thinking of the Hippocratic Oath. And nurses don't take that either."

She was wrong though. Most nurses cared more than doctors. Nurse Keller certainly did or she wouldn't be so quick to patch me up.

"So, what's it gonna be, *Doc.* Ya gonna spill all your dirty little secrets or do I have to jab a kidney next?" I smirked up at her, and she dropped the bloodied rag onto my lap, just barely covering the tenting fabric of the robe I was still wearing.

The fear I saw staring back at me had my cock rock-hard. It was a shame I wanted her to talk just as much as I wanted her to never say another word again.

"He never touched me," she whispered.

"Right... and I passed the MCAT," I grunted. She raised a questioning eyebrow, and I reached up and pulled the plastic mask off my head. That shit wasn't as comfortable as they made it look in the movies. All the sweat was making me itchy. "Ya hang around enough of 'em and you pick up a vocab word or two. Burke failed his three times."

"Four," Jules replied before she could stop herself, quickly covering her hands with her mouth.

"Okay, new girl." I grinned. "Guess there's some history there."

She shook her head again, her glare taking in my chiseled jawline and dark eyes. The tattoos that twisted up behind my ears and the hair I didn't bother to maintain when they were gonna shave it all off anyway. She hadn't noticed before with the way I'd flipped up the collar of my lab coat and kept my shoulders hiked. The hat I pulled low on my head before walking out of Briarwood that night. But I was pretty. Pretty dangerous too. But that just made me prettier, didn't it?

"No history. Us nurses just talk. Always have more to lose than our physicians do. They never mentioned you, though?" She was trying to be subtle. I didn't like subtle. Or maybe I liked it too much, and that was the problem.

"Why would they unless they were sending you downstairs..." I watched her face, waiting for my meaning to land. It seemed to breeze past her instead.

"Downstairs?"

"The basement."

"There's no—" she started to say, and I cut her off with another slap of my palm on the table.

"What the fuck did your old man do to you, Jules." I pushed up from the chair, walked over to the sink, turned on the garbage disposal, and dangled a finger over the drain. "Last chance..."

Was I really willing to sacrifice a finger just to make a goddamn point? You bet your sweet ass I was. I didn't need all ten of 'em to strangle her.

CHAPTER FOURTEEN
HIM

"D on't!" she screeched more than screamed. The sound so piercing—I hated to admit it—but I jumped back a little. Shocked, not scared. I didn't scare that easy. She stifled a sob and added, "Please don't."

"You have exactly two seconds to tell me what I wanna know, Jules, before I'm serving up minced sausages for dinner. And unlike the eggs you wasted, you will eat 'em."

"I'm telling the truth," she whispered. "He didn't touch me! My father didn't touch me..."

I believed her. Couldn't explain what it was about the woman. Could have been the fact I'd spent my entire life around liars so I recognized she wasn't one of them. At least she didn't want to be. We all had to lie when it was us versus them. When our survival was at stake.

"What he do then?" I pressed her as I switched the garbage disposal off and took a step closer. And another as I slowly guided her back down into her chair. She looked like she might faint if I didn't. Her own damn fault for washing half a body's worth of blood down the tub drain and refusing to eat.

I didn't feel sorry for her. I was annoyed at how fucking stubborn she was being.

She chewed on a nail, her other hand aimlessly tugging at the fishing line in her arm. If she was in pain, it didn't show. I flicked her fingers away from her mouth and her hand away from her stitches. Setting the knife down between us as I held her wrists in place. Not forcefully. I didn't have to be forceful when she was letting me do it.

She swallowed down the lump I could hear bubbling in her throat and plastered on a tight smile. "It was me. I did it. I didn't want to. I swear I didn't want to. But if I didn't... well, it was my responsibility. To take care of him. So I didn't argue. I didn't say no, and I don't understand why. I knew it wasn't right. It didn't feel right. I swear I didn't like it!" The words came pouring out of her, almost as if once she let one go, the rest rushed forward to follow until she was tossing a nonsensical confession at my feet.

Literally. The only thing keeping this ghost of a girl upright was my arms digging into her wrists.

I yanked her up off the floor and onto the table. I was afraid she would curl into a ball if I didn't, and then there'd be no getting nothing from her. "Him touching you, him making you touch your brother. There ain't no difference, Jules. You get that, right?" I grunted.

She was being ridiculous. Sure, I was as fucked up as

they came. But even I knew when shit was wrong. I just didn't care to be any different.

She shook her head. "He was my brother. My baby brother." She hid her face in her hands but I could still hear her rambling. "I touched my brother. Did things... And Robbie... he never got over it. The disgust I felt every time he looked at me... The disgust he showed me. Because we both knew I could have stopped it. I could have tried harder. He didn't make it to seventeen before he... He hung himself in our living room. He wanted us to find him. He wanted *me* to find him. To know why he did it."

"Makes sense." I shrugged, and her head shot up to look at me. "Why you became a nurse, not why he offed himself, Jules." I rolled my eyes. "You couldn't fix ' em. You couldn't save him. So you made it your mission to save others. Really ain't as deep as you made it out to be. Like Psychology 101 shit."

"I... that's..." She stared at me, shocked, for a moment.

"Just ' cause I'm crazy, doesn't mean I'm stupid, Nurse Keller."

"I never said you were—" she tried again.

"Didn't have to. Ya'll just assume. You'd be right too. About the crazy part anyway. But have to be plenty smart to trick ya'll into thinking I'm one of ya every few months. Fooled a few patients into thinking they were hallucinating while I was at it, and they weren't stupid either."

"So you're a..."

I grinned. "I'd give ya my chart number but they got

rid of those when they moved us all downstairs, sweetheart. Almost like they didn't want anyone to know we existed anymore. Makes it difficult to ever get released but far easier to sneak out when no one is doing nightly bed checks."

I watched her jaw drop, her eyes blink a few times, her breathing change. Leaned in and shut it the only way I knew how without a pair of underwear to stuff down her throat. I used my tongue instead. Kissing her stupider than she already looked. Pulling back and rising to my full height as soon as I felt her relax into my mouth.

She liked kissing me, and I guess I didn't hate it. Her lips tasted almost as good as her pussy.

"You were about to say it and I didn't want to hear it again," I explained with an irritated groan.

But she was still just staring at me. "Say what again?"

"*Sorry*. I told ya I'm tired of all the fucking *sorrys*. Next time I hear ya say it will be the last time I hear ya say anything, Nurse Keller." I made a slashing gesture across her throat, tapped her nose with the tip of my index finger, and turned my back on her.

She wasn't going anywhere looking the way she did. I glanced down at myself. At the pink robe. The raging hard-on. And I guess I wasn't going anywhere either. Except maybe to take a shower and calm myself down a bit.

CHAPTER FIFTEEN
HER

I watched him walk away, my lips tingling and my heart thumping in my chest, and pressed a fingertip to where I could still feel him on my mouth. The skin plump and bruised. And the next thing I knew, I was following the path he'd taken up the stairs. Down the hall, stopping in front of the bathroom.

The carpet was wet, tinged pink, and squished under my bare feet. But I crept forward anyway. Pressing an ear to the door and listening as the pipes creaked and groaned when he turned on the shower, the spray hammering against the glass enclosure before it was muffled by something stepping in front of it. Then the splashing of water. Cascading and dripping in all directions.

I didn't know why I was so curious, why I was standing in the middle of my hallway instead of running out the front door. Except I knew exactly why. I wasn't afraid, and not because I didn't think he would hurt me but because I didn't care if he did. Running was much more terrifying when you didn't have anywhere to go, nowhere you'd rather be.

I took another step and the door seemed to shift with the movement, cracking open just enough to let me peek inside. My attention glued to the image of him stroking himself. The taut muscles of his arms flexing and bulging, his eyes closed and his free hand leaving a bloodied streak against the glass. My bathroom was a crime scene in the making between the tub and the shower stall, and just like a crime scene, I couldn't look away. Each heavy breath making mine shorter, lighter, until I was gasping. Each groan making me squeeze my thighs tighter together, my teeth nearly cutting through my bottom lip.

I always knew there was something wrong with me, some sexual dysfunction that left me averse to sex since... just for as long as I could remember. Trauma-induced aversion, asexual, decreased libido, hypoactive sexual desire disorder... Each therapist *called it* something different, likely thinking changing the label would change my mindset. It didn't. I accepted sex would never be for me, and I was fine with that.

You couldn't miss what you never enjoyed in the first place.

Something was different now, though. Something shifted. Dr. Reagan would tell me it was the life-or-death experience, facing my mortality, if I were to tell her what I'd done. What I'd failed to do.

But I would never tell her. It wouldn't matter if I did, because she'd be wrong. That wasn't it. I wasn't suddenly reinvigorated. I wasn't struck dumb by the thought of dying.

I was enthralled by the idea of getting closer to it, as close as I could get to death. Teetering over the ledge, not knowing or caring which way I would go. Because both prospects were just as thrilling. Like standing in the middle of traffic and waiting to see how long it would take for one of the cars to hit you.

And that's who this man was. What he was. Death. I'd felt it when he kissed me. As warm as it was spine-chilling. I had one foot in the grave and one suspended over his shoulder until he decided to drop me.

I could also feel this pressure in my lower stomach (that was new) a flutter of something wet and warm and intoxicating as I continued to watch him. The water droplets tracing the raised lines of his tattoos, the veins of his forearms—which I could hit with a needle from a mile away—the thick meat of his thighs. I honestly didn't know if I was even attracted to men before him. But I was certainly attracted to this man. To the piece of him he switched between cradling in his hand and choking the life out of it. Twisting his thumb over the top before jerking his palm down again.

I was hypnotized. Frozen to the spot. As afraid of getting caught as I was unable to stop myself from peeking. I was a freaking peeping Tom, one of those guys who peered into windows at night and watched unsuspecting women get undressed. And as much as I knew it was wrong, I didn't care. I didn't want this feeling to end, the intensity of actually feeling something. Guilt was still better than the nothingness. I could live with guilt. I had lived with it for such a long time, but I couldn't live with nothing.

Before I realized what I was doing, my fingers were dipping into my PJ bottoms. Skimming over my lower abdomen, inching lower and lower. My panties were soaked, covered in a way I'd never experienced alone or with anyone else. I brushed my thumb over the outside of my labia, and my legs nearly gave out from under me when I accidentally grazed my clitoris.

I was more than turned on. I was close to freaking achieving orgasm. What I thought one should feel like. I let out a small whimper, which had the man on the other side of the door snapping his neck in my direction. His eyes meeting mine. Dark, unforgiving eyes. Eyes of a murderer. Eyes I wanted above me as he did unspeakable things to my body.

Instead, he just kept staring, not moving his hand. I didn't move mine either. Until he stepped out of the shower stall, stalked forward, and slammed the door closed in my face.

CHAPTER SIXTEEN
HIM

"This ain't for you, sweetheart," I called out from the other side of the door. I groaned as I gave my dick another slow tug.

It was for me, for whoever's pussy I was fucking, for whoever's throat I'd be slicing afterwards. This wasn't for her. For those sounds she was making when she'd slipped a hand into her skimpy little shorts.

I'd felt her watching me. And I'd let her do it for a while too. I'd been at Briarwood long enough to not give a damn whether or not I had an audience. That didn't mean I was gonna let her get off scot-free for spying on me.

I actually kinda liked the idea of her touching herself while she was thinking about me until she had to go ruin it by making noise.

I punched a fist in to the tiled wall, my knuckles cracking back open on impact. I'd been so fucking close and now I had to start all over again. It wasn't easy to get there when all I had was the memory of a still pussy to help me. Never did have that vivid of an imagination. Which was probably why I had such a large body count.

Take that how you want it. It worked both ways.

My limp dick twitched in my palm, reminding me I'd failed him too. Jerking off was really more of a 50/50 shot with me, and right now those odds were in the house's favor.

I dipped my head back under the showerhead, closing my eyes and cursing God and Satan just the same. Neither had done a thing for me. Then I twisted the faucet into the off position, grabbed a towel from the rack, stepped over a puddle of blood still leaking from the tub, and stomped out of the bathroom. Not stopping till I was standing bare-assed in the doorway of her bedroom again.

She flinched like I was gonna hit her, and I rolled my eyes. The damsel in distress act was getting real fucking old. Mostly because I liked it, and it annoyed me that I liked it. I didn't want to like her. I didn't want to feel a certain way when she cowered in front of me. I wanted to hate her enough to kill her. To get that high I felt afterwards, like I was fucking invincible. It was hard to feel invincible when you felt like you were kicking a puppy.

I crouched down to meet her at eye level, seeing as she had backed herself into a wall and followed it to the floor, my dick hanging between my thighs as the towel just barely clung to my waist. One quick movement and that would be on the floor too.

"Did ya like what ya saw, Jules?" I lifted a brow at her.

She hesitated before shaking her head.

"Fucking liar." I grinned and tugged her to her feet. Her wrists were oozing, and she probably needed antibiotics or something. But she was a nurse. I was sure she could figure that out on her own. "I can smell your pussy from here. You were turned on."

"I was... No, I wasn't. I'm not a... I'm not a sexual predator or anything, am I?" She was rambling again. "Oh my god! I am! I'm a predator... A deviant... I should—"

I reached out an arm and clamped my palm flat against her mouth. "Don't. Don't do that shit. Don't play victim or that's all you'll ever be." I stepped forward, pressing her against the wall and shifting my hand from her lips to brush her cheek. "Unless that's what you wanted all along. You wanna be my victim, Nurse Keller? You wanna stand here helpless while I do everything I came in here to do before I found your ass in that tub?"

And just like that, my cock had risen to the occasion. Ready to fuck this woman into the drywall. Ready to tear her in two. Ready to fold her into unnatural angles she'd never come back from.

She didn't say a word—*thank fuck*—as I wrapped a hand around the base and gave my cock a quick stroke. Hyperfocused on her face, on her wide eyes, on the way she didn't move. Working myself up to the point of no return. I thrusted into my palm, grazing her hip with each back-and-forth motion and making her head thump against the wall. I grunted and I groaned. And I cursed and I hissed. My calves aching and my breath ghosting against her skin.

I shifted my mouth closer to her lips until I was

prying it open. Forcing my tongue inside and tasting a hint of blood from where her teeth had broken through. She didn't fight me but she didn't give in either. Like that first night when she'd been unconscious, that first time I'd fucked her, and this was just as perfect.

No, it was better. Because she was looking at me.

I could feel it. See it. She was unblinking as I finally came all over my hand, pushing off the window ledge and glancing down at the mess I'd made on the pale-blue walls beside her. Then I leaned in, bringing my fingertips to her parted mouth. Feeding her what was left of my cum, painting her lips and shoving it inside.

When she still didn't move, didn't breathe, didn't say a word, I dropped to my knees in front of her and decided to return the favor.

What can I say? Emptying my balls always did put me in a better mood. Guess this time around, it put me in a giving mood too.

CHAPTER SEVENTEEN
HER

"No talking." It was the only warning he gave before he yanked down my sleep shorts and panties, and then his mouth was on me. No teeth, just tongue and lips and the bridge of his nose. Grinding and sucking and licking and doing all those things I never enjoyed. Things I didn't think I could enjoy.

I splayed my arms out on each side of me, my palms flat against the wall, trying to gain traction where there was none while his hands pried my thighs apart. Spreading me open like a surgeon cracking open a rib cage. I was just as exposed too.

I caught a glimpse of myself in the mirror across the room, my nipples peeking out of my nightshirt, my hair wild, the man crouching in front of me wilder as he grunted and huffed against my most private area.

My legs trembled and my breath hitched as that fluttering in my stomach got more intense, fluctuating between being too much and not enough. I was afraid to move while my body screamed at me to reach out and grab him. Tug him closer. Force him deeper.

And that's when he pressed something inside me, his tongue, as he made a circular motion over my clitoris with the tip of his nose. The sensation of both at once sending a current down to my feet, curling my toes and shooting back up to my lower stomach, my spine, my breasts so that every muscle was contracting, contorting and shuddering.

Then it really was too much.

I shoved at Cain's shoulders and he fell back on his ass, one eyebrow raised. "Ya coulda just tapped out, ya know. Didn't have to get violent on me."

"I'm s—I mean, I didn't know," I panted, trying to catch my breath. "That's never... I've never... Is that what it's like?"

He looked at me for a moment, cocking his head to the side. "Wouldn't know. Ain't got a pussy, sweetheart." He made a show of leaning back on his hands and eyeing me from head to toe. "Flushed face, heaving tits, thighs dripping. Looks about right, though." He grinned.

"That was... I didn't know it could be like that," I whispered, pulling my shorts and panties back up my thighs and crossing my arms over my chest. It didn't matter how many layers I had on. I still felt naked in front of him. Like he'd seen a side of me I'd never showed anyone.

I guess that was why they called it intimacy. There was just something so unnerving about someone seeing you at your worst, watching you unravel and become a version of yourself you didn't recognize—my eyes flicked towards my reflection again—even in the mirror.

"Yeah, well, my ma got one thing right," he grunted. "Taught me how to please a woman." He didn't look at me as he pushed himself to his feet and walked out the door.

He did that a lot. Walked away when something was weighing on him. He wasn't the only one, unfortunately.

"What's this?" I eyed the lump of brown meat on my plate with suspicion as Cain shoved it closer to my chest.

"It's called dinner," he grunted in reply. "I assume you've heard of it before. Eat." He turned back towards the stove and continued stirring something in a pot.

I glanced down and poked at the lump with a fork. I wasn't much of a meat eater, and there was a lot of it.

"I don't hear you eating," he barked over a shoulder, so I picked up my utensils and cut off a sliver, cringing when a pool of pink seeped out onto the plate.

"It's bleeding..."

"So were you. Now eat. You need the fucking iron, Jules."

"I don't really eat a lot of meat..." I sniffed at my fork and scrunched up my nose, at the same time Cain spun around and caught me.

He aimed a spatula in my direction, the black t-shirt hugging his arms and chest like it had been painted on.

He'd tossed his wet clothes into the dryer at some point, but they must have shrunk. There was no way he was wearing the right size.

"What? My cooking not good enough for ya, your highness? Could make ya some wine to go with it, but didn't think you wanted me hogging up the toilet for that long."

I shoved the piece of meat into my mouth and forced myself to swallow it down with a gulp of ice water. "Thought they only did that stuff in prisons?" Actually, I didn't think they did it at all. I assumed it was just something they made up for tv.

"Ain't much difference between prison and Briarwood, Nurse Keller. Give it a few weeks and you'll figure that out too." He plopped a large serving of broccoli onto my plate, next to the meat, served himself and then dropped into the chair across from me. He waited until I took two more bites, then dug in to his own food. "So you've really never orgasmed before, huh?" he said, and I nearly choked.

"I, um, I don't really think that's appropriate dinner conversation."

"Yeah, I hardly think anything we're doing here is appropriate," he countered, and I shook my head.

"I don't even know if that's what it was."

He grinned. The stupid kind of grin that made him look boyish, instead of manic. "It was."

"How do you know?" I asked and immediately regretted it.

"You really want me to tell you?"

"No." *Yes.*

"Yes, you do." He leaned forward on the table, lowering his head so that his face was level with mine. I tried to look away but it was like I couldn't. Like he was holding me captive without ever touching me. "I tasted it, sweetheart. You squirted that shit straight down my throat."

CHAPTER EIGHTEEN

HIM

S now plopped down off the top of my shoe as I kicked a boot against the lip of Jules's front door. Repeating the process with the other one till I was sure I wasn't tracking that shit into the house with me. It was cold as fuck outside but that was no excuse for ruining perfectly good hardwood floors.

See? I had manners when I wanted to. I just didn't usually want to.

I squinted my eyes and glanced at the dark, nearly-black sky and the snowflakes still falling around me. I'd tried to move the car into the street and didn't make it more than a few blocks on foot before deciding to turn my ass around.

It wasn't the best idea to leave the Wagon parked where anyone could see it. It also wasn't the best idea to spend another night here. But shit was snowed in and I didn't have a shovel—I mean, not *that* kind of shovel. Digging body-sized holes wasn't exactly in the same category as digging yourself out of a blizzard and I had no intention of scratching off what was left of the paint from my car. Rust was doing a good enough job of that for me.

I peered over at the ice covering the driveway and most of Jules's front porch. The rickety railing and the crooked mailbox. By the looks of it, Nurse Keller didn't have a hoard of spare tools holed up in her garage or a man in her life who knew how to use 'em. Chances were she didn't have a shovel hiding anywhere either.

My eyes bounced from house to house, neighbor to neighbor, snow pile to snow pile. No one was going out in this anytime soon. Me included. Thank fuck I'd ordered enough groceries to fill her pantry. We might have been stuck indoors but at least we wouldn't starve. I could go days without sleep but take my food away?

Well, let's just say there wasn't much I couldn't endure with a full belly and a pair of empty balls. And right now I had both.

I shook off my gloves, pushed my way back inside Jules's front door, and found her waiting for me in the entryway like a mutt that didn't know if it had been minutes or days since her owner left her behind.

Hint: It sure as fuck hadn't been days. But looking at Jules's face, you wouldn't know that. 'Cause the woman was staring at me as if I'd returned from war instead of the damn driveway.

"You came back," she whispered, and I *stared at her* as if she'd grown two heads. Neither of 'em were screwed on right by the way.

I crossed my arms over my chest and cocked an eyebrow. "You got abandonment issues, Nurse Keller?"

Rather than answer me, she shoved a hot cup of coffee into my hands. I had to uncross my arms to keep from dropping it as she grabbed on to my elbow and guided me over to the living room, where she had some stupid romcom playing on the television screen. The decorations and tree I'd laid out, and she'd ripped down, gone without a sign they'd ever been there.

I stopped moving when the back of my knees hit the sofa cushion and Jules shoved me onto my ass. And then she was buzzing around me, placing my mug on the table in front of us and yanking my damp hoodie off my head.

She returned a few minutes later with my spare shirt recently laundered and a platter of cookies fresh from the oven. I swiped up a lopsided circle and glanced down at the imprint my thumb made in the top. Besides the essentials, I'd ordered those premade sugar cookies that came with the little green trees stamped on the front— couldn't explain why the red and green food coloring made such a difference but it did—except these ones looked like something out of a bad baking show. More oval than round, with fork-shaped scrape marks where the red ornaments should have been.

Which told me one of two things: Jules had no experience with prepackaged cookie dough or she'd intentionally taken a knife to the tops and scratched out the designs.

I was playing house with the real-life version of the Grinch who stole Christmas.

Good thing I didn't give a shit how bad they looked as long as they tasted decent. Anything was better than Jello cups and rotten fruit.

I popped the cookie into my mouth and grinned. They were just the way I liked 'em. Hot off the pan and a little undercooked in the middle. Didn't care if raw eggs were bad for ya. Lots of things were bad for ya. Pills, alcohol, *fucking around with the girl you were pretty certain you were killing in the morning...*

I enjoyed them all anyway. Some more than others, it seemed.

Jules quietly lowered herself down beside me on the sofa, scooting over a few inches whenever she thought I was too focused on the tv to notice. Until she was practically curled up on my lap. My arm spread out across the top cushion and her head resting in the crook of my shoulder.

She was passed out before the couple on the screen had decided that the movie didn't need to be more than an hour and a half long and miraculously worked out all their issues in time for the credits to roll. Listing off all the useless fucks who still thought putting glasses on a supermodel made her ugly. It didn't. It just made her a supermodel with an eye problem.

When Jules's breathing was a mix of soft snoring and random mumbling that told me she was dreaming, I slipped my arm out from under her head and replaced it with a cushion. Then I grabbed the fuzzy blanket that I was pretty sure was as decorative as all the pillows and draped it over her before making my way upstairs to the bedroom.

I might not have needed a bed—God knew a couch was a step up from the floor—but I sure as hell was gonna use one if I had the option.

CHAPTER NINETEEN
HIM

"What the fuck are you doing?" My eyes snapped open, my hand wrapping around a tiny wrist and twisting until I heard it pop. I didn't break it but I sure as fuck dislocated the shoulder it was attached to.

Jules let out a whimper, not the scream I was expecting, as I fumbled around the nightstand, flicked on the light, and found her standing over the bed looking down at me. I let go of her arm and shoved it away, watching as it hung like a limp noodle at her side while she did nothing to fix it herself.

Fucking waste of a nursing license if you asked me.

"I just thought..." she whispered.

"You thought what? That you could just fucking grab me whenever you wanted?" I pushed off the mattress, towering above her as she shrunk in on herself. "This ain't a two-way street, sweetheart. I ain't your fuck toy. I ain't your boyfriend either."

I walked her back to the closest wall, pausing in my

steps when she was pressed up against it, and grabbed her arm. Tugging down, over, and up until I heard it pop again. It wasn't dislocated anymore but I'd bet it still didn't feel that great.

She blinked at me, and I rested a palm above her head and leaned in so that I was a breath away. Taking her wrist with my free hand, pulling it forward until her fingers were spread out over my boxers, and adding pressure to her knuckles till she was gripping the bulge there. "I already told you this ain't for you. That didn't change just because I licked your pussy a few times."

I rolled onto the heels of my feet, turned around, and stomped towards the bed, popping a Xannie before climbing onto the mattress and turning onto my side. Leaving Jules to stare at the giant skull tattoo that took up most of my back. I hoped the fucking thing haunted her nightmares like my childhood trauma haunted mine.

There was nothing worse than being woken up by a hand slipping into your boxers. I tried to shake the chill away, but it didn't help when my heart was still pounding out of my chest. That pill was doing a shit-ton of nothing right now.

Jules didn't move for a long time. But I could hear her breathing. Feel her looking at me. She should have been running scared, not padding closer to the bed again. But a few minutes later, that's exactly what she was doing. Then she was climbing in on the other side and curling up so that we were nearly nose-to-nose. I shifted back to see her face in the dim light.

"What do you want, Jules?" I huffed.

"Why?" she asked.

I rubbed a tired hand down my face. "I'm not a fucking mind reader. You're gonna have to be more specific. Why what?"

"Why won't you do it?"

"My fucking god," I grunted and pulled myself upright on the bed. "Do what, Jules? Kill you or fuck you? 'Cause one of them ain't out of the question yet."

She lifted a shoulder—the side that wasn't sore and swelled up at the joint—and mirrored my posture. "Either. Both?"

"I ain't gonna do shit if you keep asking me to do it."

She nodded a little too enthusiastically. "Okay, I'll stop asking."

"Well, now, I don't know how I feel about that either," I huffed. "Seems like you're only gonna stop asking because you WANT me to kill you."

"Okay... so do you want me to keep asking or not?" she whispered.

"Fuck... Shut up! I don't know." I clenched my jaw. "Believe it or not, killing someone who wants to die kinda takes the fun out of it."

"Is that why you do it? Because it's fun?" She wasn't being a smart-ass. I could tell by her tone she was genuinely curious. And now I had a semi tenting my boxers.

Don't ask. I wasn't really a doctor. I only played one on the weekends. Which meant I had no fucking clue where my sex drive came from. Or why this girl seemed to manipulate it with the press of a weirdly naïve button.

"More fun than when the carnies come to town." I sighed. "I do it because it's one of the few times I feel alive. Because it lets me feel in control for a little bit. And, yeah, because I fucking like it. I like the fucking high that comes with it."

I watched Jules out of my peripheral, as she wrapped her arms around her knees and tucked her chin between them. "I get that."

I turned to look at her head-on. "You do?"

She nodded. "I do."

"Okay, then can we go the fuck to sleep now?"

"You didn't answer my other question." She still wasn't looking at me, more like talking into her kneecaps.

"Because I said so," I told her.

That had her shuffling around to sit cross-legged next to me. Facing me. Those same wide blue eyes burning a hole into my forehead. "But why though?"

"Is this what it's like to be fucking married?" I muttered under my breath. Not sure who the fuck I was asking. "Look, I have a thing..."

"Like a kink?" This chick went from blushing at the dinner table at the mention of an orgasm to sex therapist in a blink of an eye.

"Sure, let's call it a kink, Jules." I shook my head. "And because of this... *kink*... Well, I need my... *partner*..." *Victim.* "To be still. Like, I mean, deathly still." *Dying or close to it.* "No talking, no moving, nothing."

"So you're a necrophiliac." She shrugged like it wasn't a big deal.

My hand shot out and wrapped around her throat. Squeezing just enough to keep her attention. "No, I'm not a necrophiliac. I don't enjoy fucking dead people. If *I* were into that kinda shit, I wouldn't need to go climbing into windows, now would I? Could find plenty of stiffs in the morgue at Briarwood."

She sucked in a strangled breath. "Okay, not a necrophiliac. Got it," she managed to force out. I dropped my hand, and she gulped down a lungful of air. "Show me."

"What the fuck do you mean *show you*?" I called out after her. But she was already gone, sprinting down the hallway and banging as she went from closet to closet in search of whatever the fuck she was looking for now.

CHAPTER TWENTY

HIM

Jules returned fifteen minutes later, dragging something down the hallway behind her. Something heavy. I slid off the bed and took a step forward to get a better look. Only to step back again.

"What the fuck! Is that a body?"

She dropped it to the floor, just over the threshold, with a loud *thud* before turning to face me. "What?" She glanced down, then over in my direction. "Oh, no. It's not real."

I just continued to glare at her.

"It's a doll," she clarified. "A sex doll."

"You have a sex doll?" I quirked an eyebrow. I wasn't judging, whether it was a doll or a body. She just didn't seem the type to have a sex, well, *anything*.

"Dr. Reagan thought it'd be therapeutic," she said, aimlessly rubbing at her shoulder. *Told ya that shit hurt.*

"And was it?" I asked her.

Jules paused, as if considering her answer. "Not really."

Then she was bending down and dragging the human-sized sex toy towards the bed like it was the next most logical thing for her to do, and I just watched her go. My tired, drug-addled brain trying to catch up with everything going on in front of me.

I wasn't sober or awake enough for this shit.

When she started hefting the doll onto the covers, I closed the distance, grumbling under my breath as I shoved her ass aside and lifted the damn thing myself.

"Okay, so what's it doing here?" I asked her as soon as I was done.

"I want you to show me," she said.

"You need to stop with all the cryptic shit and just spell it out for me like I'm an idiot," I huffed. "Show you what?"

She peered up at me, and I swear to fucking Christ there were little heart-shaped sparkles in her eyes. The kind you saw in cartoons. "How you like it. What you need to... ya know."

"Get off?" I asked.

She nodded.

"You can't have it both ways, Jules. You can't play it coy *and* have a fucking sex doll tucked away in your clos-et." I pressed two fingers to the bridge of my nose and squeezed until I could hear that buzzing sound in my temples.

If I stayed in this house any longer, I was gonna need a healthy regimen of blood pressure meds added to the roster of antipsychotics burning a hole in my backpack. Might as well add a straitjacket too.

"Just say fuck, cunt, dick, cock, pussy, orgasm, *cum*. Pick one. You're a grown-ass woman. Fucking act like it." I opened my eyes, expecting to see her tearing up again. Instead, she was smiling at me. Nearly giddy.

"So are you gonna show me or not?"

I glanced from the expectant look on her face over to the doll on the bed. More specifically at the eight-inch cock (give or take? I didn't have a fucking ruler on me) bobbing in the air. Fucking thing looked like it was waving at me every time the ceiling fan did another rotation.

"I'm not into dudes."

"Oh! Right! One sec!" She gestured with a finger before rushing towards the footboard, positioning herself between the doll's legs, one knee bracing the rest of her weight on the mattress as she used her good hand to grab and then roughly twist the rubber cock at an odd angle.

I shifted on my feet without meaning to, closing one eye as I tucked my junk protectively against a thigh. A few more quick twists and Jules had officially turned the *he* into a *she* as she dangled the makeshift dildo in front of her like a carnival prize. Except that was no goldfish flopping around in her fist.

"Yeah, that really doesn't solve the problem, sweetheart."

She tossed the cock aside—it hit something with a *thwack*—and grabbed my hand, leading me over to the footboard, and I was honestly too stunned to do anything but let her. She gestured to the doll, still grinning (Jules, not the doll; it was more ambivalent than anything else) and I followed her line of sight down to a pair of rubber pussy lips. Peach colored instead of pink, but other than that, pretty damn realistic looking.

As far as sex dolls went, the thing must have been top of the line.

"It's universal," Jules said, and this time I was the one left speechless and blinking. "Dr. Reagan urged me to be more experimental."

"I can see that." I nodded, reaching out a hand and slowly inserting a finger inside the doll's newly-altered cunt. It wasn't warm but it didn't feel terrible either. Add a little lube and it might actually feel pretty nice. "A for effort, but it still ain't really my type, Jules." I turned to look at her and watched her face drop.

"Maybe I can dress him up? Put some makeup on him?" she asked.

Maybe you could stop calling it a him. *That might really help.* But I didn't say that part aloud. "Look, I just don't think…"

"Can you try?" she begged, and I groaned.

I mean, it wasn't like it would hurt anyone. And when did I give a fuck if it did? Now, apparently.

What the fuck was wrong with me? Was I really considering fucking a sex doll just to make this chick happy?

I was, and it was doing my head in. Worse than anything else ever had.

I cracked my neck, my glare bouncing from Jules to

the inanimate doll taking up the middle of her queen-sized bed. "You got a blue marker?" I sighed, and she nodded before sprinting back out the door just like she had the first time. "And maybe a wig?" I called after her.

"Okay!" she called back.

CHAPTER TWENTY-ONE
HER

I dragged my desk chair across the room and positioned it in the opposite corner. Pausing to take in the view before realizing my error and switching it to the other side, while Cain climbed on to the bed with an exasperated sigh. He appeared hesitant—not self-conscious, not shy—when he grabbed each of the doll's legs, spread them wide, and smacked a glob of Vaseline against the rubber vagina with a loud slapping sound.

I knew he was being dramatic on purpose, like how I used to slam my door extra hard after my stepmom had finished berating me for not wearing makeup. Or wearing too much. Or not applying it right. Only I could somehow pull off both looking like a tomboy *and* a whore. The point was, dramatic or not, he was still going through with it.

I cocked my head to the side to peer around the shadow his elbow created as he twirled a finger along the rubber flaps, using his free hand to stroke his penis until it was erect, and then slowly inserted himself. An inch at a time. As though he were unsure how deep to go at first. That made two of us. I hadn't thought to test it out.

He let out a low groan when his pelvic bone finally met the outer rim, glancing over a shoulder to look at me when he thrusted forward a second time. Rough and quick. I knew better than to speak, but there were so many questions running through my mind. Questions like...

How did it feel? How much different was it from the real thing? If I acted just like that doll, would he do it to me? Could he do that to me? Would I enjoy it as much as I enjoyed what he'd done to me up until now? Would he? Or would it not be enough? Would he need to finish me to finish himself?

And why did I like watching him so much?

I didn't make a sound but I did slip off the chair and creep around the other side of the bed. Kneeling next to the nightstand and staring at the way sweat started to form between the little creases in his brow, how his gluteal muscles contracted each time he drove forward, the grunts he made—just like the ones I remembered hearing him make in the shower. Except they were deeper now, lower, more animalistic. Both louder and softer, without a door and a wall of glass separating us.

He turned to look at me again, his eyes searing into mine. I didn't blink. Didn't breathe. Even when I started to feel lightheaded. Then he was pulling me up off the floor by the wrist, still thrusting as he guided me onto the bed in front of him. The doll between us, my back pressed against the headboard, my legs tucked under me. He held my chin in place with the palm of his hand, the other arm keeping his balance. Never breaking contact, eyes or otherwise, as his rhythm grew more frantic. More frenzied. Until the doll's head was beating against my bent knees, the wig sliding and tangling in the sheets. While his movements only got harder and harder. Faster and faster. Leaving little red welts along my skin.

I couldn't hold my breath any longer, but I didn't gulp it down. I kept my respirations shallow, nearly indiscernible. My chest barely moving and my blinking in sync with his, so that every time he opened his eyes, mine were already there. Staring back at him. An optical illusion that had him entranced and the sheets beneath me damp. A mix of sweat and bodily fluids that left my thighs slick.

I was aroused. Almost as aroused as he seemed to be, as aroused as the stress lines on his forehead told me that he was.

It didn't hurt that I liked looking at him. I liked seeing myself the way he saw me. What he saw I couldn't tell you but it was enough to have him fighting his urges while giving into them at the same time. Proving that if you were patient, you could have your cake and eat it too.

His fingers pressed harder against my jaw, bruisingly hard, his teeth clenched and his nostrils flared. I'd recognized that look, the moments before a man ejaculated, the few fleeting moments that were somehow worth everything it took them to get there. And I never understood it. What was so great about it. Never cared to.

Now, I couldn't imagine anything more enthralling,

anything more hypnotizing than witnessing the way *this man* gave himself over to pleasure. How he wanted me there with him, experiencing it both as an outsider and an equal participant.

Yes, it was sex, a release of endorphins. But it was something else too. It was him sharing the darkest part of himself. Indulging and trusting me.

I didn't care how messed up it was, just like he didn't seem to notice how messed up *I* was. And I wanted him. I wanted to keep him. To keep this feeling.

His thrusts had slowed, long and languid, as he drove up into the doll. Just as fiercely as when the headboard was banging against the wall, without the same desperation, though. Almost as if he'd been worried he wouldn't get there if he didn't do it quick.

But now he knew. We both knew. We could both sense it.

Two more thrusts and he finally released his grip on my chin, dropping his palm to the mattress and collapsing on to the doll's chest with a satisfied groan. And I didn't feel sick. Or dirty. For once, I wasn't disgusted. Because he hadn't done this to me and I hadn't done it to him. We'd done it for each other. Because I'd asked him to do it, and for whatever reason, he'd agreed to try.

I counted to sixty in my head, like I was taking a heart rate—mine was off the charts—before finally mustering the courage to speak. "How was it?"

He lifted his face off the doll and glared at me for a long moment, his eyes narrowed. "You were better."

CHAPTER TWENTY-TWO
HIM

I could go again. All she had to do was look at me, and what was left of my blood was rushing south. I didn't know if that was a good thing, or the worst possible thing. I didn't know what it'd mean if I was never fully satisfied. If the high didn't last me a few months like it used to. If this was temporary or a permanent affliction. If she was the disease or the cure.

I shoved the doll aside, reached out an arm and tugged Jules down the bed by an ankle. She panicked, her arms flailing and grabbing at the sheets before she settled herself and I drove up into her with a single thrust. Her pussy wet, gushing, throbbing before I'd done anything but impale her.

The doll was fine. The doll got me there like my palm got me there, like my fantasies could sometimes get me there. But this was different. This was warm. This was flesh. This breathed and bled, suctioned and swelled.

I didn't know if she was bluffing. If she really wanted me to fuck her or not. Though the tears streaming down her cheeks hinted that it wasn't what she thought it would be.

"What's wrong? I thought this was what you wanted? To be my dead girl? My little doll? Sure seemed like it was what you wanted when you were watching me." I clamped a hand down over her mouth. I couldn't chance her answering me. I couldn't be sure what I would do if she did. I couldn't be sure how I'd feel afterwards.

And right now, all I wanted to feel was the way her pussy was constricting around me. Her muscles pulling me impossibly deeper. It wasn't the stillness I was used to. The stillness I thought I always needed. Somehow it was better. The heat, the tension, the shallow breaths steaming up the palm of my hand. I tried to concentrate on that, instead of the fact I was going off script.

Honestly, it wasn't that hard when my cock was *that hard*. Fucker was doing the thinking for me.

My thighs were aching, my neck kinked as I forced myself to keep watching her face. Staring into her eyes and waiting for them to close. To blink. To tear up or flicker. They didn't do any of that. She wasn't crying anymore. Just reflecting the image of me leaning over her back at me. Thrusting in and out. Diving farther and farther into the abyss there was no returning from. The one she wasn't supposed to return from either.

A few more drives of my hips into her tight cunt, the smell of pussy juice and sweat filling the air, and I couldn't help myself. Something was missing. That metallic scent I was so used to. The added heat that came with it.

I yanked her head to the side. Exposing that long, pale neck. Jules needed to get out in the sun more. Guess that was what happened when you worked nights, though. Your skin got deathly white. The blood loss probably didn't help much with that.

I wanted to bite down, rip into flesh, see the red I remembered draining from her wrists. Feel how wet and warm that was too. I wanted to penetrate her in more ways than one. I could picture myself doing it. As vivid as if it were happening in front of me. That last gasp of air she would take, the way her chest would stop moving while I kept *moving*. Thrusting, fucking, obliterating her insides until they were spilling out between us. On the sheets, my hands. That pale skin getting paler.

It was the part where fantasy blended with reality. Where the control I had was the biggest turn-on of them all. Where life and death blended together and you didn't know what was what anymore.

Fuck, maybe I did like them dead. Maybe I needed more than just the quiet and stillness. Maybe there was never going to be the perfect one for me. Because they weren't dolls. Jules wasn't a doll. Eventually she would bleed out. Eventually those eyes wouldn't be watching me. Because they couldn't. They would rot out of her skull. Turn gelatinous. Change color.

They always did.

I couldn't deal with the decay. When they stopped looking human and started melting into lumps of meat and curling flesh.

I also couldn't get out of my own head. Couldn't focus on anything but the inevitable and how different it felt while also feeling exactly the same. Like dropping a glass bottle off the roof. Didn't matter whether you were watching it or not. You'd still hear it shatter. Pretending otherwise wouldn't change its fate. And it wouldn't change Jules's either.

She was as broken as that bottle and so was I.

"Fuck!" I yelled it out loud this time, shoving myself back. My cock sticking to my thigh, wet and limp. My hand clutching a knife I didn't even remember grabbing. For fuck's sake, I didn't even know where the fuck it came from.

I'd blacked out. At some point while I was fucking her, I'd blacked out. I was moments away from stabbing her. I didn't know what stopped me. Or if it changed anything. What I did know was that I didn't like the way she was looking at me right now.

Not scared. Not angry. But like she fucking pitied me. Like she wanted to do whatever she could to fix me. And that just meant we belonged on the same side of the looney bin.

CHAPTER TWENTY-THREE
HIM

I paced back and forth in the living room. I was crawling out of my skin. I needed to *get out* of here. The snow was finally melting, but I couldn't bring myself to push through the front door. They should have been looking for me by now. They probably were. But that wasn't why I didn't want to leave. Why I couldn't leave.

It wasn't just the snow storm that had caged me inside these walls. It was something to do with this woman. The way she clawed her way into my head. The last woman to have done that... well, I'd give ya one guess. She certainly wasn't someone I cared to see again, even if I'd never stopped seeing her.

I popped a couple more pills and forced them down with a glass of water from the kitchen sink. At this point, I only had a few days' worth burning a hole in my pocket. I hadn't gone without 'em for as long back as I can remember. Since the day I was dragged out of that temporary foster home and left to rot in a cell at Briarwood. Wasn't even sure if I needed 'em, just that I liked the way they seemed to dull everything around me.

I could hear her feet padding across the floor. I could sense her watching me long before that, though. Like she was trying to decide if she should approach me or not. If she wanted to. Which was both smart and dumb in equal fucking measure. Didn't take a genius to know that what she should be doing was staying far the fuck away from me.

"Are you okay?"

The question was so ridiculous I dropped the glass into the sink, lifting a curious brow when it didn't shatter before turning back in Jules's direction. "You tryin' to be funny, sweetheart?"

She shook her head, her eyes just as wide as the first time I'd seen her walking the halls at Briarwood. Like a pinkie mouse dropped in a den of snakes.

"No, I'm not the fuck okay. Haven't been okay in a real fucking long time, Nurse Keller. But ya knew that before ya asked, didn't ya?" I mumbled under my breath, digging around in my pocket for another Xannie, only to come up empty. "Fuck..."

"What's wrong?"

Jules stepped closer. She reached out an arm and I snatched it up before she could make contact, rearing back to take a look at her wrist as soon as something wet brushed against my skin. The wound was oozing. Not blood either. Pus. Greenish and clumpy. Shit was infected. It was starting to smell too.

"What the actual fuck? You just gonna let your arm

rot off? What kind of nurse are you?" I shoved her arm back towards her chest and rubbed a hand over the fuzz on my head. She was rotting away, walking around but not any less a corpse than the bags of human meat I'd buried. As if the rest of her hadn't realized she was dead yet.

She glanced down at her wrist, clutching it to her chest before peering up at me again. "I need some antibiotics, a few sutures, but it's not bad."

I didn't know who she was trying to convince, me or herself. Neither one of us seemed to believe it.

"You need something too, don't you? What are you taking?" She offered a palm and waited. Watched me.

I shoved past her and headed for the living room. Crouching in front of my backpack, fishing around for a few moments, then drawing out the little orange bottle that was tucked at the bottom. The staff didn't exactly like coming downstairs every day, so those of us who weren't chained to bedpans were tossed a handful of pills every few weeks and left to fend for ourselves. Made for horrible compliance and fantastic currency.

Hey, whatcha got there? Oh, I'll give ya ten of these peach-colored ones for five of the blue.

Fuck no. Make it fifteen and you have yourself a deal.

Not always the way it went. Sometimes shivs were involved—discarded syringes were the worst 'cause you never knew what was in 'em—but you catch my drift.

I tossed the bottle in Jules's direction. It landed at her feet and she bent down to grab it. Running her eyes over the label before looking back at me.

"These are antipsychotics. Do you need antipsychotics?"

I couldn't tell if it was fear or concern I heard in her voice. Maybe a mix of both. Didn't know what she was expecting from a mental patient. Wasn't like I was locked up for daydreaming.

I shrugged a shoulder while pushing to my full height to tower over her again. "Depends who ya ask, sweetheart."

She nodded once. "Okay, what else?"

She didn't have anything stashed around the house. I would have found it already if she did. Which meant Miss Goody Two-shoes was thinking about raiding the drug closet.

I cocked an eyebrow at her, without bothering to ask the question.

"You said it yourself. I need antibiotics and you need these." She shook the empty bottle as if she were trying to justify her actions. She didn't have to justify shit to me. I was surprised. That was all. "So what else?"

"A few bars."

"Bars?" she repeated.

"Xannies, Jules. As many as you can grab without raising alarm bells." I had to admit the confused look on her face was cute. She nodded before I added, "And don't go in the basement. Nothing good's in the basement."

She turned to walk away. I grabbed her wrist—the oozing one—and tugged her back in my direction.

"I mean it."

She peered up at me for a long moment, but she didn't flinch. Like she found me more interesting than scary and that was a problem. For her as much as it was for me. I'd make her afraid if I had to. It was what was best for both of us.

"You were in the basement," she finally replied.

"My point," I grunted before shoving her towards the door. "Nothing good."

CHAPTER TWENTY-FOUR
HER

The halls were quieter than I remembered them being. *I know what you're thinking. Quiet was good, right?*

Not on the psych ward it wasn't. No, it wasn't good at all. It was suspicious. Spine-chilling. Or maybe I was just projecting. Since nothing was more suspicious than the way I was sneaking through the pharmacy door and flicking on the light.

It wasn't locked, which was odd too. Though I'd been warned that if you didn't yank it closed hard enough, the lock wouldn't catch like it should. It was a problem no one seemed too keen on fixing, and I wasn't here to stir the pot, just shove some narcotics and as many benzos as I could grab into my pockets. Antibiotics too.

I wasn't sure how necessary the clozapine was, but I wasn't going to argue with Cain. A quick withdrawal would have him feeling worse, believing he needed it, when really his body had grown dependent on it—whether or not it should have been prescribed.

Truth was, it was probably meant to subdue him and his system had just adjusted to the dosage. He was a big guy, and big guys needed more than what he was getting... if he needed them at all. I wasn't a doctor. I just cleaned up after them. Spotted their mistakes and brought them up as delicately as possible without ruffling anyone's feathers.

I scanned the shelves until I found what I was looking for. These 25mg tabs would have Cain feeling "normal," while a slight titration would leave him sedated, especially when mixed with the benzos he was swallowing like candy.

It wasn't just bad practice to have all the bottles out in the open like this. Most hospitals had some sort of automated dispensing system by now. Type in the patient's name or chart number and document and assign the correct medication. No manual counting, less of a chance of someone disguising theft as "human error..."

I shook my head. It wasn't the time to shift into nurse mode, even if it was my default setting in this uniform. I glanced down at my light-blue scrubs. The color was supposed to be calming for the patients. Instead, it felt like waving a red flag in front of a bull. It didn't matter what you wore when you were shoving pills down someone's throat. Nothing was going to make them feel better about what you were doing, even if you were honestly trying to help them. And I did want to help them.

I also wanted to help *him*. I didn't know why. Or maybe I did and didn't want to admit it. *Probably that.*

None of it changed the fact that I wanted to help Cain. Worse was the guilt weighing down my shoulders as I stepped out of the pharmacy and back into the hall.

My motives were selfish. Because I wanted him to help me too.

It was why I was risking everything coming back here after calling out for the week. I said I had the flu. Couldn't bring that onto the unit or it would spread like wildfire. And the only thing us nurses wanted to deal with less than an unmedicated patient was an unmedicated patient aspirating on the prescriptions we were trying to feed them. It was a step up from bedbugs or a lice outbreak but not by much.

I tugged on the door until it clicked closed behind me, grateful that my keycard wasn't the last one to swipe inside, before glancing to my left and then my right. Nothing but silence and emptiness staring back at me.

A few lights flickered overhead in that eerie way they always did. Old wiring and old walls. Unless you believed the rumors about the place being haunted. I didn't. More because I didn't want to believe them. I had no desire to be proven wrong, though.

I made it to the main reception area before the freight elevator caught my eye. I had to admit I was curious. Not curious enough to go down there but curious enough to pause in my steps. There was no one behind the counter and no one manning the security desk. Which again was as lucky as it was not all that unusual, depending on who was on shift. I might not have been employed here long, or much longer if someone caught me walking out the front door with a uniform full of stolen medications. But I'd already picked up on the fact that hospital protocol was much more theory than practice at Briarwood Sanitorium.

Never leave the pharmacy unlocked, unless you forget to pull it closed. Then pray no one rats you out.

Never leave the registration counter unsupervised, unless you need a cigarette break. Or to run out for lunch. Or because Hare called you into his office. Or because we're understaffed. Then don't you dare bring it up.

Always change linens in pairs, unless you're a male orderly. Then by all means, creep into female patients' rooms whenever you like.

There was that chill again. The one crawling down my spine, especially when my eyes caught on the elevator for a second time. Each of the numbers on top lighting up one by one as the cable car slowly made its way from the basement to the lobby.

I gasped without meaning to, tucked my hands into my pockets to ensure I still had everything I came for, and then rushed out the employee entrance, to where I'd left my car idling in the parking lot.

There were cameras everywhere, meaning there was no guarantee I'd gotten away with anything. But they were rarely pointing where they were supposed to be pointing. Not that I was all that worried about losing my license with everything else Cain said was going on behind the scenes.

Was it dumb to believe an escaped psych patient pretending to be a doctor so he could climb in through my window (or how ever he got in) to murder me?

Maybe. Probably. But it felt worse not to believe him.

He had no reason to lie to me when he was being so honest about everything else. I'd take an honest asshole over a charming snake any day of the week. Sure, both could sneak up on you, but at least one of them had the decency to warn you they were coming.

CHAPTER TWENTY-FIVE
HIM

I didn't believe in ghosts. Was pretty certain if they existed, there would be hordes of them following me around. The restless spirits of all the women I'd put into the dirt. Instead of just one. This one.

I glanced across the table at my mother. That smug smirk on her face as she stared at me over a cup of vodka that didn't exist even though I could smell it. My stomach twisted as I took another sip of black coffee, hoping it would help. Phantom odors were the worst. You could close your eyes but you couldn't do shit to plug up your nostrils.

"Knew you were useless but never took you for stupid." She looked me dead-on when she said it. Another reason I knew she wasn't real. My mother never looked at me. *"Letting that girl leave. She's probably talking to the cops right now, leading 'em all right back here to you."*

It was just my brain's way of fucking with me. Telling me what I was already thinking because why the fuck not trauma dump while I was at it?

"Probably." I shrugged a shoulder, returning my attention to the little screen in my hand and scrolling through Jules's socials on her phone—I was smart enough to keep that.

She didn't have anything interesting on here. No family photos. No dirty laundry out in the open. Just a few bullshit affirmations and a handful of selfies of her smiling. Not her real smile. The kind you made in those corny-ass school pictures that had you looking more constipated than happy. She didn't even have any interesting messages in her inbox. I'd snooped through all those too.

Chick had less of a social life than I did, and I'd been locked up in a nuthouse since I was ten.

"So you want the electric chair? That it?"

"We both know there ain't no death penalty in Illinois." I laughed, and yeah, I realized I was laughing at myself. Couldn't help it if I was fucking funny.

A loud banging on the front door had that laughter dying in my throat as quick as it had started.

"Told ya." My mother hummed to herself, clinking her spoon around her mug. Pretending it was tea when I could smell that it wasn't. *"No reason for the girl to knock on her own door."*

I rolled my eyes, pushing up from my seat before heading to the entryway.

"You ain't gonna answer it, are you?" She called out after me.

"Why? Afraid your ghost won't look good in orange?" I called back over a shoulder.

Then I reached out an arm and yanked the door open.

It was cold as shit outside but you wouldn't have guessed it from the way I was leaning against the frame in nothing but a pair of low-slung sweats.

"Can I help you?" I grinned at the little prick taking up half the front step. Didn't look like a cop, but what the fuck did I know about how cops were supposed to look? Everyone was always more interested in picking my brain than arresting me. At least they were when there was only one body tied to my name. Could be a different story now.

"Where is she?" The guy tried to look past me, into the house. I moved myself over another inch to keep him from seeing anything other than a wall of tattoos.

"Who the fuck are you?" I quirked a brow at him, crossing my arms over my chest as I watched the fucker watch me. I was a big fucking dude. He wasn't.

He swallowed once before trying to puff himself up like some sort of over-inflated peacock. "Pretty sure I should be asking you that. Now where's my Jelly Bean?" I stared at him like he was stupid and he clarified, "Juliet."

"Not here." I lifted a shoulder, while the fucker tried to step past me. There was nowhere for him to go.

"Mind if I check?" he asked.

"Actually I do. But I'll be sure to let 'er know you stopped by." I stepped back as I grabbed hold of the door, preparing to slam it shut. Guy definitely wasn't a cop or he would have been flashing his badge already.

He kicked out a shoe, resting it on the threshold. I glanced down at it. I should have broken his foot. But I wasn't looking to cause a scene where the neighbors could witness it. I tugged the door all the way open again and waved at some prick walking his dog. He stared at me for a moment and finally waved back. He didn't know me. It was just something people did when they were afraid of coming off rude.

Then I returned my glare to the shoe that was dripping wet snow onto Jules's clean floor. Didn't know why it annoyed me but it did. So I leaned forward until I was eye to eye with the guy. "You might wanna move that before I move it for ya." I didn't raise my voice. I didn't need to. There was nothing more terrifying than the calm before the storm.

"Not until you tell me where she is," he grunted.

I threw my head back on a laugh. "I don't answer to little pricks like you. Neither does Jules."

He frowned at me for a moment. Taking me in from head to toe. Usually that was the first thing people did when they looked at me. But this time, I think it was the nickname that did it. "Who the fuck are you?" he tried again.

"*Jelly Bean's* boyfriend," I said, and the fucker stepped back like I'd slapped him across the face.

"My sister doesn't have boyfriends," he mumbled more to himself than to me.

"You're right. I was being polite. We just fuck a lot." I grinned, only to immediately drop it. "Wait? What the fuck did you just say?"

"My sister—"

"Yeah, that's what I thought." I didn't let the fucker finish speaking before I was tugging him inside and slamming the door closed behind us.

CHAPTER TWENTY-SIX
HIM

"Did you just fucking piss yourself?" I grunted, using the tip of the kitchen knife to guide the fucker's legs farther apart and get a better look at the area around his crotch.

I didn't remember his jeans being so dark. I didn't remember him smelling like an outhouse neither. A boys' locker room maybe, but not an outhouse. There wasn't enough cologne in the world to cover up the stench of insecurity. And this guy was bleeding that shit from his pants.

"You did, didn't you?" I laughed as he mumbled something incoherent from beneath the tape I'd had no choice but to slap over his mouth as soon as I dragged him into the living room and he'd started screaming like a little bitch.

I was being a good houseguest, keeping Jules from getting a noise complaint against her. Unlike some people, I was fucking considerate.

"You gonna stop with the screaming?" I quirked a brow at him.

His head moved up and down a few times in response, and I tugged the duct tape off with a quick flick of my wrist. Shit stuck to my fingers. I shook out my hand, closing my fist over the rolled-up ball it made and tossed it aside, before returning my glare to the prick with a *wet prick* sitting in front of me.

"Sure hope you're a man of your word or this ain't gonna go well for you, Robbie." I aimed the knife at him for emphasis.

"Ow, fuck," he hissed under his breath, making faces as he loosened up his jaw muscles. When he was finally done fucking around, he peered up at me. "Where's Juliet?"

"Already told ya... She ain't here, pal." I tapped my index finger against his temple. "You slow or something?"

He watched me move around the back of the chair he was tied to out of the corner of his eye. I placed a hand on each of his shoulders, never letting go of the knife, and squeezed. Harder than was friendly or necessary.

What can I say? The guy irked me. I didn't like being asked the same dumb-ass questions over and over again. Probably had something to do with my upbringing. Quacks loved asking the same dumb-ass questions a million different ways. Come to think of it, cops did too.

"What did you do to her?" Robbie asked. Though it didn't seem like he really wanted to know the answer.

"Nothing she didn't like," I replied. "Wasn't lying when I said I fucked her. A lot."

"I don't believe you."

I circled back around, tugging a second chair forward so we were sitting knee to knee. Or more like knee to shin. Mine were much higher than his. Fucker was bite-sized. Must have run in the family. Because Jules was bite-sized too.

I had no intention of putting this particular Keller anywhere near my mouth, though.

"Yeah, and why's that? Don't think I'm pretty enough?" I rubbed a hand over my chin, over the stubble that was growing along a very-square jawline—Holly-wood worthy if ya asked me—and leaned back in my seat. One arm draped along the top rail, the other resting on my lap with the sharpest part of the knife jetting out between us.

If looks could kill, my brains would be splattered all over the far wall as this fucker laser-focused his glare on the center of my forehead. Like he could already picture the bullseye there.

"My sister's not like that," he said.

"Like what?" I laughed. "A dirty little whore who likes to suck cum off my fingers? 'Cause I can assure you she is. Don't think you know 'er as well as you think you do, *Robert*."

He tilted his head to look at me for a moment. "I know her a hell of a lot better than you do, asshole."

"That so?" I leaned forward again, elbows digging into my knees. My face so close to his I could smell the nicotine gum on his breath. *Quitter.* "Why because your old man made ya diddle each other when you were kids?

Hate to break it to you, but that don't make you an expert on the woman."

Now this fucker was the one grinning. "That what she told you happened?"

I didn't like being caught off guard. Didn't like the way it made me feel. Didn't like to believe she'd lied to me. And not just about this fucker being dead but about what happened between 'em.

I could look past a little white lie. One little white lie, but two was un-fucking-forgivable. Two changed it from a mistake to a pattern of behavior. Two made it easier to do it again. That was how I ended up the way I did. With so much blood on my hands.

"She did, didn't she?" He was laughing in my face, throwing his head back as far as it could go and laughing. His Adam's apple bobbing up and down like a fucking worm on a hook. Except my teeth were sharper than any fish I knew. And so was the fucking butcher knife I was clutching in my hand.

It was all over the news, every radio station and media outlet blasting a minute-by-minute update. Cops were arriving in droves. Streets were closed off and sirens were wailing in the distance. I kept my head down and hoped that Cain was doing the same.

He wouldn't go outside, would he? It wasn't like he had anywhere else to go or I was sure he would have gone there already. Still, I had this sinking feeling in the pit of my stomach, and I didn't have my phone to warn him...

Not that it mattered if I did, since he didn't have one either. At least I didn't think he had one. Exchanging numbers didn't exactly come up in conversation when you were sharing your space with a serial murderer. Assuming he was one. I didn't know how many people he'd killed. Or if the total made a difference...

I sighed and slammed the trunk closed. I also didn't know what I was walking into, but the car I saw parked outside my house told me it wasn't going to be anything good. I should have known someone would show up as soon as word got out. I guess I just assumed I had a little more time.

Maybe that was just wishful thinking on my part. I *was* pretty good at ignoring a problem and hoping it would go away on its own.

"Shoot, shoot, shoot..." I cursed under my breath. It was my own fault. I should have left the hospital and came straight here, instead of making a pit stop at the closest department store. It was the girl at the register who'd asked me if I heard about what had happened at Briarwood.

Of course, I hadn't. Until I got back to the car and flipped through the radio stations. And now it was too late. All I could do was face the problem head-on.

"No more hiding, Jules," I told myself, smiling at the nickname. I liked it. I liked when he said it. I liked him. Even though I knew I shouldn't. I also liked doing things for him.

I glanced at the four bags of clothes currently weighing me down as I climbed the stairs to my front door. I was trying to do something nice so Cain didn't have to keep washing the same two pairs of underwear and socks every other day.

Instead, I was walking myself into a war zone. I knew it the moment I pushed the door open—like the pharmacy, it wasn't locked—and dropped the bags next to the little console table where I stored my keys. Then I took three hesitant steps forward, gasping as soon as I crossed into the living room.

"Welcome   home,   sweetheart,"   Cain   crooned,

gesturing the knife in his hand towards the slumped figure he had taped to the chair beside him. "I assume you know our guest? He certainly knows you." Cain pushed to his feet and then he was stalking towards me, blood dripping down his hand with each step he took in my direction. "Or should I say *knew* you..."

My eyes flicked from him to the chair, then back again. "What did you do?" I whispered, though I wasn't sure why I was asking when the answer was staring me in the face.

"You told me your brother was dead." Cain jerked a single shoulder. "Now he is."

The hair on the back of my neck stood on end. He'd never looked at me like this. So detached, so out of his head. Like all the humanity I'd seen before had seeped out of his pores, joining the puddle of blood on the floor. Robbie's blood.

I didn't remember moving, stepping back, but I must have because suddenly my spine was pressed up against the wall. My head turned to one side and my hands out in front of me. They wouldn't stop the knife but they would slow it down a bit.

"It's better than the alternative. Me accepting the fact that you lied to me, Jules." Cain inched closer, stopping when we were sharing the same air as he leaned forward and sniffed my hair. "You wouldn't do something like that, would you? You wouldn't be so dumb as to lie to me, right?"

I shook my head from side to side, finally turning to look at him again. "I didn't lie... I swear."

He grinned. But he wasn't smiling. "The body in that

chair says otherwise, sweetheart." He flicked the knife behind him before aiming it back at me.

"I didn't lie," I repeated because I didn't know what else to say.

Cain lifted the knife, stabbing it into the spot right next to my head. Catching a lock of my hair and embedding it into the wall. Then he lowered that same hand to my face, tapping his index finger against the tip of my nose. "You said he hung himself."

"And he did!" I nodded, forcing down the part of my heart that was thumping in my throat. "He just didn't die. Because I found him and—"

"And what, Jules?" Cain interrupted at the same time he was asking me to finish speaking.

"And I cut him down."

"You hear this shit?" Cain laughed. But he didn't appear to be talking to me anymore. He was looking past me. Into the kitchen. The empty kitchen. No one else was here, except me, him, and... no one else. Dead people didn't talk back. "Guess I was right," Cain said, returning his attention to me. "You got a savior complex, don't you? You get as much of a high from saving a life as I get from ending one."

"No, I don't." I shook my head. "I'll prove it to you."

"Yeah, and how you gonna do that, Jules?"

I'd already lowered my hand, wrapping my fingers around the syringe in the front pocket of my scrubs. Then I quickly tugged it out and jabbed the tip into the meatiest piece of flesh I could reach at this angle. Hoping like heck my plan would work.

And if it didn't? Well, I was okay with that too.

CHAPTER TWENTY-EIGHT

HIM

"What the fuck did you just do?" I grunted, staring at the needle currently sticking out of my arm before looking back at Jules. At her wide eyes and flared nostrils.

"Exactly what you asked me to do?" she replied between heavy breaths.

"Pretty sure I didn't ask you to stab me with whatever the fuck this is." I wrapped my fist around her hand and squeezed until she loosened her grip, then I yanked the needle from my skin and tossed it aside.

"It's just another benzo," she whispered. "Little higher dose to counteract the tolerance you've built up."

I could already feel my eyelids getting heavy. I shook my head and blinked a few times. "I can't believe you fucking drugged me."

Was it hypocritical as fuck? Sure was. But we'd already established I was more of a do as I say and not as I do sorta guy.

I stumbled back a step, my ass hitting the sofa before my entire body slid down the frame.

Little higher? Yeah, don't think so. This chick hit me with a fucking horse tranquilizer.

I glanced into the kitchen to find my mother grinning at me. She didn't have to say it. I already knew what she was thinking because it was what I was thinking too.

Told ya so.

I must have drifted off because one long blink turned into lost time. To the clock on the wall telling me almost an hour had passed and I was still sitting on the floor in the living room. I wasn't dead, though. So, shit was looking up.

I shifted my weight onto one arm and tried to move but the rest of me wasn't having it. I was still so fucking tired...

When I opened my eyes again, a handful of minutes later, I found Jules standing over me. Two of her fingers resting on my neck, her attention on the clock, and her lips twitching slightly without realizing she was doing it as she counted in her head.

"Just checking your blood pressure," she said the moment she turned back around and saw me staring at her. "You were out for a while."

"Ya don't say," I hissed.

She flinched at the edge in my tone but she didn't step away. "I was just trying to help you relax so we could talk."

I let out a low, humorless chuckle. "Doesn't get more relaxed than knocked the fuck out, now does it, Nurse Keller?"

She stared at me for a few seconds, her eyes watering. And suddenly I was left feeling bad again. This shit was getting real old.

"Go on, then. Talk." I sighed. "I'm listening."

She nodded once before sitting in front of me cross-legged on the floor like we were about to have a fucking tea party or something. And my ass was highly under-dressed.

"I never wanted to be a nurse, you know?" she admitted. If she expected it to be some big "got ya" moment, it wasn't.

Lots of people ended up doing shit they never wanted to do when they were younger. *Take me, for example. Serial killin' wasn't exactly on my list of career choices but here we were.*

"Okay?" I prompted her.

"I didn't like people. Still don't really like them or understand them. But animals are different. Animals were never as difficult to understand for me. I wanted to be a vet or open my own animal shelter—"

"That's great, Jules. I like puppies too, but—"

She kept talking over me, staring past me, instead of looking at me. "Which was why I was super excited when our parents took us to a petting zoo. Robbie was nine. I was eleven. It was the first time I'd ever seen someone milk a cow in real life…"

"Glad you're feeling so chatty and all, but what does any of this have to do with—" I tried again.

She cut me off. "You said you wanted the truth, right?"

"I sure as shit don't want you to lie to me," I ground out between clenched teeth.

"Then let me finish. This is the only way I can do it."

"Go on then," I huffed. "Tell me more about these… cows?"

"Did you know that if you don't milk a cow, infection can set in and she can actually die? It's called mastitis. Her udders become engorged and the pain is excruciating. Like getting kicked in the testicles times ten."

I winced, peeking one eye open while squeezing the other one shut at the thought. "Okay, great. I get the picture. And?"

"*And* not long after that demonstration at the farm, Robbie began sneaking into my room. Told me how people weren't that different from cows. That sometimes they needed to be milked too."

"He fucking didn't…" I tugged myself straighter, my hands clenching into fists at my sides. I didn't feel guilty about gutting the guy, but I sure as hell felt a lot better about it now. Guess my instincts were right.

"He did. But it was my fault." She shook her head. "I was older. I shouldn't have been that naïve."

"That was not your fucking fault, Jules. You were a fucking kid," I reminded her.

"So was he. And he was my baby brother. It was my

job to take care of him. And I did. For years. Until I started to question if I was doing something wrong. Because it felt so... wrong, Cain. I knew it was wrong and I kept doing it anyway."

I reached out a hand to wipe the tears from her face, one palm flat on the floor to keep myself from tipping over. I didn't have words for her. There was nothing anyone could say that made that shit better.

She shook her head again, and I didn't know if it was because she was arguing with herself or the version of her brother she saw in her mind. Whether it was victim or villain, I couldn't tell ya. The brain was funny like that, always trying to make sense of the fucked-up shit that didn't make sense. Always trying to justify it.

"Robbie insisted it was okay. Told me that *Dad* said it was okay. That he wanted me to do it. All big sisters did it. They just didn't talk about it. That worked for a while too. See?" She took a deep breath and finally met my gaze. "I wasn't lying when I said my father made me do it. To me, it was the truth. For a long time, it was *my* truth. I honestly believed I was doing what my parents expected of me. I didn't like getting in trouble. I never had a rebellious streak. I just wanted them to be proud of me. But that sick feeling never went away. Ever."

That made two of us.

"So I told Robbie I was going to talk to Dad, ask him if what we were doing was wrong or not. I just needed a little reassurance. To hear it from someone else. Not even twenty-four hours later, my brother tried to hang himself. On Christmas morning. Right in front of the tree, knowing how much I liked to get a peek before everyone else was up. And when I found him, after I cut him down, he said he wouldn't make it so easy to save him next time. That he'd write a note telling everyone it was my fault for taking advantage of him."

Jules choked out a sob, and I tried to grab on to her. Tug her close to my chest. She just shrugged me off and scooted farther back on the floor.

"I never brought it up again. Never acknowledged what we did. What we continued to do, *after* he married Natalie. I never spoke about it to anyone. Not even to him. I just shoved it all down as deep as it could go until I didn't feel bad anymore because I didn't feel anything anymore. Until you forced it to come back up again in the kitchen that first time."

"That's... fucked up." *Fucked up* didn't cover it. But there wasn't a word for what it was. It was fucking diabolical.

"What's the difference?" Jules countered. "You were gonna kill me."

"Yeah, but you're not a kid anymore."

"And that makes it better?" She lifted a challenging brow.

"The only thing that separates us from those animals you love so much is the ability to decide which lines you won't cross. Mine is kids."

"Mine is killing people," she mumbled. "In case you didn't notice, I suck at it. So thank you for doing it for me." I cocked my head to look at her. She must have sensed my question without me ever having to ask it because she added, "Robbie. He needed to be put down."

"Yeah, and why's that?" I wasn't arguing with her. I was just curious as to her reasoning all of a sudden.

"His wife told him she was pregnant. And my brother... he told her that he hoped they had a little girl who looked just like me," Jules explained. "You corrected the mistake I made when I cut him down. So, like I said, *thank you.*"

CHAPTER TWENTY-NINE
HIM

e had a body to take care of, a bathroom that still resembled something out of an episode of CSI, and a duffle bag now full of stolen drugs. Meanwhile, Jules was acting like everything was peaches and fucking cream. Disassociating was a common coping mechanism and this girl was an expert at it.

I wasn't half bad at it myself. I just wasn't interested in spending the rest of my life in a jail cell to keep from dealing with my issues. *Our issues?* I guess they were our issues now, weren't they?

I scratched my forehead with a knuckle. *When the fuck did that happen? When did* me *become a fucking* we?

Shortly after she became an accomplice to murder, most likely.

After changing into the clothes she'd brought back with her, which I had to admit I was grateful for, I found her humming to herself in the bedroom, bent over the mattress as she finished creasing the edges of the sheets.

I leaned against the doorframe and watched her for a moment. At the very least, she did seem lighter. Not exactly the reaction I expected when I'd admitted to offing her brother but it was nice to feel appreciated for once.

"Whatcha doin'?" I asked, pushing off the jamb and walking towards her.

"Changing the sheets," she replied, glancing back at me over a shoulder. "I wanna try something."

I paused in my tracks. "That so?" Last time she wanted to *try something,* I ended up almost killing her, and I realized I didn't want to do that anymore. At least not to Jules.

She was one of the few people to not look at me like I was a monster. And the others? The only reason they didn't look at me like that was because they were monsters too.

Maybe we could be platonic roommates or something.

"I want you to try having sex with me again." She grinned, and my dick jumped in my sweats.

Okay, maybe platonic wasn't the right word.

She inched forward to touch me, and I grabbed her wrist. Gently. "I don't think that's a good idea, sweetheart."

She looked down at where I was holding her, then back up at me. "Why not? Am I not... Are you not attracted to me?"

Fuck. Me. I wished that were the problem. Would have made this shit a hell of a lot easier.

I dropped her wrist and grabbed her face between my thumb and index finger. *Not so gently.* Then I lowered my head to hers, brushing my lips over her mouth. She smelled like clovers—a mix of vanilla and honey that was neither. She also smelled like blood. But she wasn't bleeding. Not from anywhere I could see. And I'd showered twice since our... situation in the living room. Which meant the odor wasn't coming from me.

I pulled back and took a step so that I could look at her. All of her.

"What's wrong?" she asked.

I leaned forward and sniffed at her again. Didn't know if I was smelling things or if she could smell it too. I also wasn't sure I wanted to know the answer. Ignorance being bliss and all that shit people liked to say.

"Blood. I smell blood, Jules. You bleeding somewhere?"

Her cheeks turned a bright shade of red, not blood red, but close enough to it. "Ah, yeah. That's why I wanted to try something."

Look, I was a guy. A guy without much life skills outside the walls of a looney bin. A guy who hadn't lived with a woman besides his mother—outside a brief stint in foster care—since I was eight. So it took longer than I'd like to admit for shit to click.

"You want me to fuck you on your period?" I wasn't disgusted by the idea. Obviously a little (or a lotta) bit of blood didn't bother me none. I was just trying to figure out where she was going with this.

She nodded once. "I took a beta blocker."

I pointed to myself. "Not a real doctor, remember?"

"Right, okay." She nodded again, dragging the chair

out of the corner and into the middle of the room before gesturing for me to sit.

I plopped down, crossing an ankle over a knee as I watched her climb onto the bed to position herself in front of me.

"Beta blockers lower blood pressure. For someone with normal ranges—someone like me—they can have a stronger sedating effect. Less pressure on the heart means less chance of bleeding out... you know, if I should accidentally get cut or something. But it also dehydrates you," she explained. Though honestly she wasn't explaining much of anything to me. "Menstrual fluid is very... um, lubricating."

I dragged the chair forward a few more inches. "Still feel like I'm missing something, sweetheart?"

"Another few minutes and I won't be able to fight the fatigue anymore." She scooted herself towards the middle of the bed, crossing her hands over her lower abdomen while staring at the ceiling. "My heart rate will get so low it'll be like I'm almost dead," she told me, her voice already sounding heavier than usual.

"What the fuck?" I jumped off the chair to lean over her, straddling her waist on the mattress while bracing most of my weight on my thighs instead of her lower body. "This your way of trying to off yourself again?"

She shook her head, staring up at me with those eyes —eyes I couldn't fucking resist, no matter how hard I tried—her chest barely moving anymore. But it was still moving.

"What if you don't wake up?" I asked her. I didn't

even know if she could hear me or if she was too far gone already.

"There's an EpiPen in the nightstand," she whispered. "If I don't wake up on my own, use it. Won't be as effective but should be enough of a jolt to make sure I'm breathing. If that doesn't work, use my phone to Google how to perform CPR."

"Are you fucking kidding me?" I glanced from her face to the nightstand. "You want me to fucking Google CPR?"

This time, she didn't answer.

CHAPTER THIRTY
HIM

I had to admit she looked pretty dead. She also looked *pretty,* dead. Her hair spread out around her like a dark halo, her eyes unblinking—just barely open—her every muscle perfectly still. A piece of rare meat set out in front of a predator.

And I was fucking starving. My mouth watering and heart beating erratically with that jolt of adrenaline I got right before a kill. It had me feeling both on edge and eerily calm as I stalked around the bed. My eyes flicking to the EpiPen on the nightstand without realizing they were doing it.

Never used one of 'em before but the instructions seemed simple enough. Besides, I was great at stabbing shit.

I stopped walking when I made it to her head, lowering a hand to her lips where the lightest breath bristled my fingertips before shoving my thumb inside, feeling the wetness that welcomed me there. She didn't move. Didn't acknowledge that I was touching her as I continued to thrust my thumb in and out of her mouth a few times.

Then I stepped aside, tugged her sweatpants down her legs, and did the same thing to her pussy. Inserting a finger, circling it around, and then drawing it back again. The translucent pink film coating my skin. Sticky with a tangy odor my nostrils recognized as easily as it recognized the blood mixed with it.

I lifted my thumb to my mouth and sucked it clean, my cock twitching in my boxers as this new flavor danced across my tongue. It didn't taste like I thought it would. The period blood diluted the pussy juice or maybe it was the other way around. Either way, I could taste the bite of both. At the same time, I couldn't distinguish either.

I yanked my shirt over my head, tugged my boxers off my ass, and kicked the pile of clothes aside. Before jumping on to the bed. Jules's body bounced with the added weight, settling against the mattress as I settled myself between her spread thighs.

She was either really fucking out of it or that fucking good at pretending. I raised my hand to her neck, leaving a streak of red behind. She was warm and she had a pulse. Barely. But she was the nurse here. I was just some guy who'd traded a handful of pills for a stolen lab coat. I was also the guy about to fuck her unconscious body because she asked me to do it. Because some sick part of her wanted me to do it. Wanted me to need her, I guess.

That part would take some getting used to. This was different from the doll she'd shoved under the bed when we were done with it, different from when she was trying her damnedest to stay still. But it was very much like that first time I'd touched her.

I lifted her wrist, gripping her just below her stitches, and watched it drop to the bed without resistance. Dead weight. And then I was grabbing on to her thighs, yanking them down the mattress and spreading them wider as I dove in. Cock-first into her warm cunt. Tugging her hips up to meet me thrust for thrust.

I was wrong. This was different from that first time too. Because I wasn't nearly as hesitant. Nearly as unsure about what I was doing or why I was doing it.

I wanted this. I wanted her. And she wanted me too.

I threw back my head on a loud laugh, knowing I sounded manic even if no one was around to hear me. No one but Jules and she wasn't hearing much of anything.

Or maybe she was hearing it all and didn't care enough to comment.

Didn't matter because I wasn't stopping as I thrusted forward again and again. All my focus on the way her cunt felt against my cock, how her eyes were looking at me from under her hooded lashes. Like even in her unconscious state, she couldn't keep herself from looking at me. I couldn't keep myself from looking at her either. From watching the way her tits bounced, then slipped to the side, bounced and slipped to the side. Back and forth. The smell of blood and cum filling the air and mixing with the sweat rolling down my spine and dripping into my ass crack.

She let out the smallest moan, and I froze. Glancing up at her face. She didn't make another sound. Didn't move and I realized it had been involuntary. Me fucking her forcing the air in her lungs out of her parted mouth.

I readjusted my grip on her meaty thighs, shifting my hands up an inch as I yanked her forward. Once, then twice, pelvic bone meeting pelvic bone as I stuffed my cock as deep as it could go without cutting her open.

I liked the way this felt too much to cut her open...

I also liked the way her insides coated my cock. Red with darker, fleshy clumps splattering off my balls and painting the sheets until I was covering it all with the white of my cum as I quickly pulled out and finished all over the side of her thigh.

I stared down at the mess I'd made. The crime scene I'd created all over her blankets. It was morbid. And it was erotic. It was also the most beautiful fucking thing I'd ever seen.

I dropped her legs back onto the mattress and plopped myself down next to Jules on the bed, turning to look at her as she continued to look straight ahead.

"That was fucking fantastic," I told her before stretching an arm across us and snatching up the EpiPen. "Keep this up, sweetheart, and I might not have a reason to revive ya."

It was the truth. I had the perfect balance of life and death resting in the palm of my sticky hand. My thoughts of using it warring with the desire to fuck her again.

CHAPTER THIRTY-ONE
HER

I was thirteen years old when I realized you didn't *have* to put a horse down after it broke a leg. It was a choice. Because it cost too much money, time, energy to repair a break. But that wasn't all. A fractured limb left the poor beast susceptible to infection and the list of comorbidities that came with it. Laminitis, abscesses, gastrointestinal issues...

Horses were bred to be agile, fast. Large torsos and thin, brittle legs meant they had difficulty moving around when you took one of those legs away. They couldn't rest the bone long enough to heal. Then it became a matter of quality of life. What kind of pain the creature would endure during that healing process and if it would be indefinite.

Mother nature was cruel. But sometimes she was kind too. Sometimes death was the kindest thing you could do for an animal you couldn't fix.

Robbie was that animal.

I'd tried for years. Did everything I could think of to

try to fix what wasn't right with his brain. And I only succeeded in prolonging everyone's suffering. Including my own. Because I'd failed him as much as he'd failed me.

I saw that now. I saw it that night I put a razor blade to my wrists. Except I'd taken the easy way out and attempted to put down the wrong beast.

The truth was, I would have been a horrible veterinarian. I didn't have it in me to make those hard choices doctors had to make on a daily basis, and my baby brother? He was my weakness. He always had been and I couldn't live with the guilt anymore. The nothingness it turned into. But Cain didn't have to be like Robbie. He wasn't broken in the same way. He still had a chance to heal and I wanted to be the one to help him do it.

The sex doll wasn't the answer. I realized that too. But maybe incapacitating myself was. Maybe it could be...

I didn't feel the jab of the injection tip, but I did feel the sudden jolt of epinephrine flood my system. My heart beating faster as the beta blocker fought the artificial rush of adrenaline. Like two steam engines colliding head-on. It was enough of a shock to send me into cardiac arrest, except it didn't.

Instead, I sucked in a gasp of air, my eyes fluttering open as sweat drenched my forehead. I closed them again and took a few deep breaths, trying to block out the sensory overload that had my body feeling like it was under attack. Until I sensed him standing over me and my nerve endings ignited in a different way. My thighs clenching together and my pale skin turning flush. I didn't have to see it when I could feel my cheeks burning up.

I didn't know what it was about him. But this man had this habit of making me feel alive even when I was dead...

CHAPTER THIRTY-TWO
HIM

I watched her face for a lot longer than I cared to admit, the little expressions she made as she came to and then went somewhere else entirely. Didn't know where. Just that it wasn't here. With me. And I didn't like feeling like I was sharing her with someone or something. Even if that something was in her head.

My feet hit the floor with a loud thud as I twisted off the bed, pulled open the bedroom door, and stomped downstairs. It didn't take long before I could sense her following me. Slowly. She was still shaky on her legs, holding on to the banister for dear life as I kept my back to her.

A little voice in my head was telling me I should reach over and help steady her before she missed a step and went tumbling down in front of me. A much louder one was reminding me that the last thing I should be doing was touching her when my bruised ego was itching to bruise her too.

I'd made it to the kitchen, throwing a pan on the

stovetop while clanking around in the drawers by the time she caught up with me again.

"You're mad at me," she said it like it was some sort of declaration. It sure as shit wasn't a question so I didn't see a need to answer her.

The chair scraped against the linoleum flooring as Jules pulled it from the table and sat down. Watching me as I brought the water in the pan to a boil. We both needed the carbs for one reason or another so spaghetti and red sauce was what she was getting. Whether or not she cared for it, I didn't *care*.

There was only so much I could do in the kitchen. Wasn't like Briarwood offered home economics. Most of this shit I learned how to do by watching YouTube videos on a stolen phone.

"Why are you mad?" she tried again.

"You asking me or telling me this time?" I grunted as I broke the pasta in half and forced it past the bubbling surface with the tip of the spatula. I was half-tempted to use my hand, just to relieve some of the tension in my shoulders.

Getting a nut off was supposed to help relax ya, not wind ya up worse. Right now, I was one of those racecars you pulled back over and over, and I was just waiting to shoot across the ground as soon as my wheels touched dirt.

When she didn't answer me, I turned around to find Jules staring out into the living room. Her focus hooked on the fucker sprawled out on the floor.

"If ya wanna be with him so bad, you're more than welcome to go over there, sweetheart," I told her and waited for her reaction. I meant it too. If she wanted to go where that guy was going instead of being here with me, I had no qualms about sending her there.

She shook her head before meeting my glare. Her eyes watering like she'd changed her mind and wasn't feeling so appreciative anymore.

I slammed a palm down on the counter to get her attention, and she curled her arms around herself. Pulling her feet up onto the chair and hugging her knees. "I keep expecting to look over and find him... I don't know... just gone..." she whispered.

I peered over at the living room with a smirk. Fucker wasn't popping up like some jump scare. That shit only happened on the big screen. In real life, dead guys stayed dead.

"I promise you he ain't going anywhere." I twirled the spatula around before withdrawing it from the pot and gesturing the fat end towards the blood that was making its way into the hall, a large dark puddle already seeping into the carpet. "Feel free to check for a pulse if ya don't believe me, though."

She shook her head again.

"Good, then go on and set the table. Dinner'll be ready in thirty."

She opened her mouth to argue, and I was quick to cut her off.

"Don't wanna hear that you're not hungry. You're fucking eating."

Thirty minutes later, Jules was sitting across from me with a bowl full of pasta in front of her, just like I said she would be. Never saw myself as a feeder before this but it seemed the more reluctant this woman was to eat, the more I was inclined to pile up her plate. Besides, she was too skinny. I wasn't into chicks who counted calories. I wasn't really into chicks I wasn't tying up either—until now, I guess.

She set her fork down after taking a handful of bites, and I mimicked her movements. Though mine was more of a slam than a clank. "What are we gonna do with him?"

She was peering into the living room again, and I was fucking tired of being passed over for another guy. Especially a guy who wasn't nearly as good-looking. Dead or alive.

"What do ya think we're gonna do with him, Jules?" I threw back at her, snatching up my fork and stuffing my face with as much pasta as I could fit without choking. I wiped the excess sauce off my chin and licked my fingers clean.

Fuck her manners. My dinner. My rules.

Nothing I did seemed to bother her though. Not even the slurping sounds I made as I sucked another strand of spaghetti into my mouth and finished it off with a burp.

That finally caught her attention, her eyes wide as she looked at me. But it wasn't with the judgement I was expecting to find. It was desperation. "Can you do it now? I want him gone."

I reached an arm across the table and pushed her plate closer to her chest. "I'll clear my schedule as soon as you clear your plate."

CHAPTER THIRTY-THREE
HIM

"Pass me the bone saw." I extended an arm, waiting until I felt the familiar weight of metal in the palm of my hand. To my surprise, Jules didn't hesitate.

I got that nurses weren't exactly squeamish. But this wasn't any old lump of meat I was dismembering in the middle of her bathroom floor. It was her brother.

"You don't have to be here, you know," I grunted as I popped his arm out of its socket and began working on the other side. They made this shit look easy in the movies. Truth was, it was fucking exhausting.

When she didn't respond, I glanced over a shoulder to find her shaking her head at me.

"Suit yourself, sweetheart." I shrugged. "But I ain't about to keep it pretty for ya."

When I started removing his lower intestines, depositing them into a black trash bag, Jules rushed over to the toilet and wasted the nice dinner I'd just made her. That was something else movies didn't tell ya. All the different odors that came with dissecting human flesh, depending on what part you were cutting into.

Bone smelled like Doritos—the red kind you could get out of the vending machine at Briarwood. Brain matter smelled like pennies and the tofu they kept at the nurses' station whenever Burke was on a crash diet. And the spinal cord... well, that took me a while to figure out. But the best way to describe it would be like the over-salted crab meat I got at the diner a few years back. Didn't know if it tasted the same and had no intention of finding out either.

My guess it was the rotten stench of Robbie's bowels that had gotten to Jules, though. I had an iron stomach and even I could feel the acid burning my throat.

She wiped a hand over her mouth before turning around to face me. The forced smile did nothing to cover how queasy she looked. "Sorry."

"I'm not the one going to bed hungry now."

"Food is the last thing on my mind," she muttered under her breath as I chucked one of Robbie's legs into the tub to drain.

It wasn't my best clean-up job, but seeing as Jules's little stunt had already left a pink ring around the ceramic rim, I wasn't as concerned about keeping shit tidy as I'd normally be. I also had the luxury of taking my time with this one.

At least until someone came looking for him. Which reminded me...

"How long we got before that wife of his calls the cops?" I turned around and cocked my head to the side, watching the way Jules was twisting the hem of her shirt in her hands. She was nervous about something.

Then again, for most people, being nervous was normal when dead bodies and cops were thrown into the mix.

She shook her head again instead of answering. I cocked an eyebrow and she added, "She won't."

"Yeah, and what makes you so sure about that?"

Jules crossed her arms over her chest, straightening her spine before immediately curling in on herself. "I just am."

She wasn't lying. That was something I learned in the short time I knew Nurse Keller. I'd been right. She didn't lie. She just didn't always tell the entire truth. Lucky for her, all I cared about when my hands where covered in blood was the part she *was* telling me. No one was showing up on our doorstep looking for the guy I'd spent the last few hours chopping up and sectioning out.

I rinsed my hands in the sink, tied off the black trash bag, and tossed it over a shoulder. I had some street dogs to feed. It was the best way to get rid of the organs.

It was also something Jules and I had in common. She wasn't the only one who told the truth. *I* wasn't lying when I said I liked puppies.

I made it to the bottom of the stairs, Jules trailing silently behind me before a knock on the front door had me glaring over a shoulder at her. She shrugged, her eyes wider than saucers as she shoved past me to peer out the peephole.

I released the bag with a loud sloshing sound and rushed after her.

Was my shirt still tacky with blood? Sure was. But one of us was good under pressure and it sure as shit wasn't the one of us who'd flushed their insides down the toilet a few minutes ago.

The cop spun around just as I swung the door open with an easy smile on my face. Enough for him to think I wasn't hiding anything but not enough for him to see Jules pressed up against the wall on the other side.

"Something I can help ya with, officer?" I called out over the sound of the sirens wailing in the distance.

He looked at me, at my relaxed posture, and relaxed himself before his glare hitched on my hand resting against the frame. I followed his line of sight, quickly lifting my thumb to my mouth and sucking it clean.

"Cranberry sauce." I grinned. "Bitter but the wife loves the stuff."

He watched me for another moment. Kid was young. Younger than me. Smaller too. He wasn't looking for trouble any more than I was right now.

"Honey," he replied, then quickly added, "My ma's recipe. The only way I can stomach the stuff."

"I'll have to try that." I nodded while doing my best not to appear too antsy. I glanced from him to the caravan of cop cars lining the street. "The parade coming early this year?" I said, and it seemed to take him a second to realize what I was asking.

"Oh, ah, no." He removed his hat and scratched the back of his head as he took a few tentative steps forward. Which told me he'd been hoping I didn't answer the door as much as I was regretting opening it. "I'm guessing you haven't been watching the news?"

"Can't say that I have. Too busy cooking up Christmas dinner." I gestured a hand behind me. Towards the kitchen, where nothing was cooking but the BS I was spewing in this pig's direction. "Would you like to come in? There's more than enough to go 'round."

" 'Preciate it, sir. But you know how it is. Got citizens to protect and serve." He tossed his hat back on his head and tipped the brim at me, before reaching out an arm to shove a flyer in my hand. "Just passing this along."

My eyes bounced from the grainy face of the guy on the flyer to the stoic expression of the uni standing in front of me. "This something I should be worried about, officer?"

The kid appeared to consider his answer, his nerves having him balancing from one foot to another as he seemed to fight the urge to look towards the cop car idling behind him. "Ah, no," he finally said. "Doubt he could make it out this far on foot. It's just a precaution. You know, a reminder to keep your eyes open and give us a call if you see anything out of the ordinary."

I shoved the flyer into my back pocket, never dropping my grin. "Will do," I replied as I watched him turn around and make his way towards the next house.

CHAPTER THIRTY-FOUR
HIM

The moment the door clicked closed, I twisted the lock and latched the chain in place. No one was getting in *or out* right now. Then I pivoted on a squeaky heel. My sneakers covered in a mix of bleach and dried blood.

Thank fuck I didn't have to lick those clean. I could still taste Robbie's bodily fluids on my tongue, and they sure as shit weren't as appetizing as his sister's.

"Tell me I'm wrong, Jules." I aimed my murderous glare at her. "Tell me you weren't keeping shit from me again. Because unless I'm as dense as that fucker out there..." I threw an arm towards the window. The curtains drawn tight so that the only one who got to witness the full extent of my irritation was the girl chewing on her bottom lip like looking innocent was going to do her any good.

It wasn't. We both knew it too.

"Unless I've really lost my goddamn mind and all this is a figment of my imagination, unless I'm not just seeing and hearing shit but feeling it too…" I extended an arm and touched her. "…you didn't seem all that surprised to find a cop on your front step handing out *these*." I tugged the faded mugshot photo from my pocket, flattened it out as best I could, and shoved it in her face, tapping an index finger against my temple as I closed in on her. "Am I *crazy* or does this guy look kinda familiar? And ya know what? His name sounds kinda familiar too?"

Without a word, she ducked under my arm and made a run for it. Leaping over the trash bag I'd dropped in the landing and sprinting up the stairs. I shook my head as I watched her go.

Never made sense to me why people did that in all the horror flicks. Running up the stairs instead of out the back door was no more useful than a rat placing its own tail in a mousetrap. But I wasn't gonna complain when I was the guy with a rodent problem.

I took the steps two at a time as I chased after her, making it to the bedroom at the same time she tried to slam the door in my face. I grabbed on to the jamb with one hand and pried the door back open with the other while my foot kept her from closing it all the way.

"Will ya stop fucking around," I grunted as I tracked her from one corner of the room to the next as she pinged like the lights in a pinball machine. "I'm not gonna hurt you."

She didn't stop moving until she found what she was looking for, spinning to face me with something shiny in her hand, the hot end of a metal barrel leveled at my chest.

On instinct, I raised my arms, palms out, as I slowly

inched in her direction. She wasn't gonna shoot me. At least I didn't think she was. Then again, I didn't think she was the type to have a gun either.

Nurse Keller was full of surprises today.

"I just wanna talk, sweetheart," I tried again. I kept my voice even, much calmer than the pounding in my head, than the throbbing in my dick. I got off on her fear, not on the fact I was two seconds away from having my brains splattered all over the carpet.

I also didn't know what was good for me any more than she did.

"No, you don't." She shook her head.

"Yes, I do." I drew a lowercase T over my chest with the tip of my finger. "Cross my heart and hope to die." I grinned. Jules didn't.

Tough crowd.

I backed up until the underside of my knees hit the mattress, and I dropped down onto the bed. "So were ya ever going to tell me?"

She nodded, her hands shaking so much I was afraid she might shoot me without meaning to.

"How about we put the gun down now, sweetheart."

"If I do that, you're gonna leave," she croaked, tears silently streaming over each of her cheeks. She tried to wipe them away without lowering her arm and nearly succeeded at shooting an eye out.

I extended a hand, gesturing for her to give me the gun. "I'm not gonna leave. Promise."

She stared at me through watery lashes for a long minute, likely trying to figure out if I was telling her what she wanted to hear or not.

I wasn't. I meant it when I said I wasn't gonna leave her. Especially when I realized why she'd run up those stairs. She wasn't trying to get away from me. She was doing whatever she could think of to keep me here.

I should have felt as trapped as that rat. I should have been doing whatever *I could* to chew my own tail off. Instead, I was curious.

Probably a little flattered too, if I were being honest. And at least one of us needed to be honest if we had any hope of getting out of this mess without ending up in a pair of matching jumpsuits.

She gently placed the gun in my hand and took a step back. I didn't let her take another before I grabbed her wrist and tugged her into my lap. Cradling her like my mother had never done to me. Not even as a newborn. Because she was too busy getting high and I was too busy convulsing. But I did my best to fake it.

I could feel someone watching us in the background. Disapproving blue eyes, twisted lips, and a shake of a head. I ignored her. If I kept ignoring *her*, she'd go away.

"I gotta take care of the trash bag." I sighed into Jules's hair when she finally stopped sobbing. She had a little residual blood splatter there. Other than that, she smelled like her shampoo.

"But you're coming back?" she whispered against my chest.

"Yeah, Jules. I'm coming back," I told her. "But first I wanna know how fucking long your brother's been a patient at Briarwood."

CHAPTER THIRTY-FIVE
HER

I tried my best not to fidget with the lanyard in my hands as Nurse Adams escorted me down the long hall of doors. Past Robbie's room as we made our way towards the pharmacy. It had taken every string I could pull to get him transferred to Briarwood, more favors than I could count to get myself assigned to his unit as a new hire. But he was my baby brother, and I wasn't about to abandon him now.

It was my own fault, really. The reason he was here. Whether that meant in a psychiatric hospital or on this earth was anyone's guess. Both were true.

The bump of my chest against someone's back had me pausing in my steps and Nurse Adams turning around to glare at me over a shoulder. "Please pay attention, dear." She tsked her tongue. And the pet name wasn't as endearing as it sounded. "Not sure what the patients were like where you're from, but one wrong move could mean life or death at Briarwood."

I nodded, swallowing down my anxiety, as she shifted a few orange bottles aside on the shelf before grabbing the one she was looking for. "I'm always very careful with administration," I assured her. "I double— triple check labels, ID bracelets—"

She cut me off before I could finish speaking. "Med errors are the least of your worries, Ms. Keller. It's not *their* lives at risk," she grunted, her lip curling at the mention of the patients. "It's yours."

Not everyone was in this line of work for the right reason, not even me. Yes, I wanted to help people. But more than that, I wanted to help Robbie. And myself, I guess. I wanted to feel better about myself. I wanted to feel...

I must have been staring off into nothing again, because Nurse Adams snapped her fingers in my face before brushing past me. I rolled my eyes and followed her. My stepmother had always said rolling your eyes was rude but so was snapping your fingers. So we were even now.

My reluctant chaperon didn't stop until we were standing outside Room 202. Robbie's room. Nurse Adams then snatched his chart from the bin outside his door—most hospitals would have everything electronic, not Briarwood—her glare flicking from the name in front of her to the name on my new employee badge. It wouldn't take a genius to figure out we were related. But that was another thing about Briarwood; you learned not to ask questions. If you were here, in this building, on this floor, it was because someone higher up on the food chain wanted you here. In this building, on this floor.

It was more than likely the same person who signed your paycheck. Silence wasn't cheap, but it sure as heck was lucrative when you knew how to keep your mouth shut. Something Nurse Adams seemed more than willing to do as she shoved the chart into my chest and handed me the little paper cup of medication.

"I assume you can handle this one on your own?" She lifted a challenging brow at me.

I nodded and watched as she spun on a heel and clicked her way back down the hall. They were irritated clicks. But I wasn't here to make friends. I was here to make sure Robbie was taken care of, as best I could in a place like this. Either way, it was better than the jail cell they were trying to toss him inside before throwing away the key.

I knocked once, using my badge to swipe into his room. He swung his legs off the bed and took two steps forward, his hands clasped behind his back as I closed the distance.

"Fancy seeing you here, Jelly Bean." Robbie grinned, appearing way too happy for the guy who'd just been charged with murdering his pregnant wife and unborn child.

I took a deep breath and schooled my features. I loved my brother. I really did. More than was good for either of us. I just didn't understand why he'd done what he did. I wanted to. I wanted to believe he was out of his mind. But somewhere deep inside, I knew he was just manipulative. It was much easier for him to tell the judge, his lawyer, the media that he was crazy than it was to admit he was just... evil. That he didn't want to be a father to a baby *boy* any more than he wanted to be my brother.

It didn't matter. He was family. The only family I had left and it was my job to take care of him.

"How are you feeling?" I asked, forcing a smile as I extended the cup in his direction.

"Better now that you're here," he hummed, knocking it out of my grip and sending the medication flying across the floor. And then he was the one closing the distance. A single predatory step at a time.

"I'm at work, Robbie," I tried to reason with him, my left hand scrambling for the knob, for my badge, as soon as my back hit the door.

"And we have a private room all to ourselves," he hummed. "*Sis.*" He slapped a palm above my head, loud enough to have me flinching, the other pressing the door closed as he ground himself against me. "I have an itch that needs scratching. I'm in pain, Jelly Bean."

I squeezed my eyes shut like I always did. Pretended like I was somewhere else as he tore at my tights, yanking them down my thighs before he was dropping his pants.

It was the last time I wore a white tunic to work instead of the blue scrubs I was issued that day. It was also the last time I went into Robbie's room without a male orderly behind me...

Nurse Adams didn't ask what had taken me so long

or why my makeup was running down my face when I returned to the nurse's station nearly an hour later. But like I said, she was paid to not ask questions and I'd spent decades acting as though I had nothing to report back anyway.

BONUS CHAPTER
ROBBIE

My Jelly Bean was in one of her moods again. Calling out of work and holing herself up in that little townhouse of hers. She always came to her senses though. Realized there was nothing closer than family.

This time wouldn't be any different. Big sister couldn't stay away from this dick. And it couldn't stay away from her either.

I reached a hand into the waistband of the cheap-ass scrubs the lovely state of Illinois had issued me and adjusted myself.

Other than the shit food and scratchy clothing, this place wasn't as bad as they made it out to be. And it was a hell of a lot better than a jail cell. Plus, there was a lot more pussy 'round here than any prison I'd heard of. Fine-ass pussy attached to long-ass legs and a set of jiggly tits.

I watched the red-headed one scurry by the little panel cut into my door a lot faster than usual, her face flush and her eyes wide, and adjusted my dick again. Juliet wasn't the only one with a hole worth fucking. These nurses loved a good sob story, and I had plenty of them I could dish out.

My wife cheated on me.

The pressure of providing for a newborn drove me to do it.

I wasn't in my right mind when I found out we were having a boy (and not the bouncing baby girl I'd been promised).

It didn't matter how much any of that was true or not. Because these dumb bitches wanted to believe the lies. They wanted to believe that the only way a guy like me—good looking, decent family, pleasant demeanor—could do something so heinous was trauma. And I was an expert at pretending I had a shit ton of trauma.

I didn't. I was just born with a few screws loose and I had no desire to tighten them.

Truth was, while my big sister was rescuing baby birds from their fallen nests, I was off somewhere dissecting their mother. Watching the way she flapped and squirmed and pecked until she finally stopped moving.

I stepped away from whatever was going on in the hall and turned back towards the single barred window. Not that there was much to see out there other than the rows of creepy white crosses that lined the hill. Probably should have put a chill down my spine or something. All they did was pique my curiosity as to what kind of twisted shit I could get up to without anyone caring enough to look.

They sure as hell didn't care about how loudly the

door was rattling the other day, the sounds Juliet made, or how long she was in my room instead of making her rounds.

The door swung open and my lips tipped up into a smirk, only to drop when I saw some crippled kid staring at me from the threshold. I recognized him from our group therapy sessions. Other than that, I had no fucking clue what he was doing here.

He crooked his head to the side while eyeing me up and down a few times. "Aw, don't look so disappointed. Bet I could blow ya better than that stuck-up sister of yours."

I raised an eyebrow. Not because I was interested but because it had only been a handful of days and my secret was out. I didn't give a fuck. Murder, incest, neither made much difference to me. Couldn't say the same about Juliet though. She liked keeping our reindeer games under lock and key and I liked keeping her under my thumb.

"Unless you got a cunt hiding between those rickety legs, you can fuck right off, Tiny Tim," I grunted at the kid.

Instead of flinching, the fucker laughed. Guess I forgot I was dealing with a bunch of crazies.

My gaze dropped to the pair of crutches he was leaning on before flicking to his shaved head and almost-white hair. "Didn't you used to be in a chair?"

"Didn't you used to have a wife?" He swung out the duffle bag in his hand and tossed it in my direction. I watched it land in front of my slippers with a thud that told me there were at least a pair of shoes and some keys inside.

"What's all this?" I muttered under my breath as I set the bag on the bed and unzipped it.

"A fucking unicorn." The kid rolled his eyes. "What does it look like? It's the shit you came in with."

I glared at him over a shoulder. "Yeah, and you're just giving it to me out of the goodness of your heart?"

I tugged out my jeans, a shirt, a pair of shoes with their laces intact and my house keys. Along with my wallet and cell phone—the cops had returned it when they realized they weren't gonna find anything I didn't want them to find on there. But that wasn't all. There was also several pill bottles lining the bottom and a few packets of nicotine gum.

I would kill for a smoke...

"What do you want for this?" I asked, because I was certain the kid wanted something.

I'd been here long enough to realize this place worked on a barter system. I'd also been here long enough to know nobody had shit worth taking until now.

The kid shrugged before tossing me a keycard he must have snatched off one of the orderlies. "We need a distraction, and you look like the kind of guy who's good at... distracting..."

I glanced from the kid, back to the bag. A private room was great, considering the alternative, but my freedom was better.

I flicked the keycard between my fingertips. "Does this get me outside?"

The kid grinned. "Sure does."

Twenty minutes later, I was strolling out of Briar-wood and over to the old BMW I found parked to the side with the keys still in the ignition. I adjusted the seat and the mirrors, running my tongue along my teeth as I gave my reflection a once-over and tossed a piece of gum into my mouth. And then I turned onto the gravel path that led me away from the iron gates and towards the main road.

I had a couple of hours before the nurses found a pile of pillows tucked into my bed and the cops were on my tail. But in the meantime, I might as well pay my big sister a visit.

BOLO

FIRST DEGREE MURDER, SUSPECT IN MULTIPLE HOMICIDES

ROBERT EDWARD KELLER

KNOWN ALIASES:

"Robbie", "Edward", "Eddie"

LOCATION:

Current location unknown. Last known location is the parking lot of Briarwood Sanitorium.

CONTACT:

Anyone with information is asked to call the Chicago FBI Office at (312) 555-5555, or your local FBI Office or Law Enforcement Agency.

SUSPECT DESCRIPTION:

Robert Keller is wanted in connection with multiple homicides that took place at Briarwood Sanitorium over the weekend. Keller was under the care of the staff, pending his upcoming trial, in which the suspect was charged with the first-degree murder of his wife and unborn child. Suspect is considered armed and extremely dangerous.

Keller is further described as the following: 23 year old white male, brown hair, blue eyes, may or may not have facial hair, approximately 5'7" and 170 lbs.

ARMED AND DANGEROUS

Chicago Tribune

Briarwood Sanitorium first opened its doors in 1915 as a treatment center for tuberculosis.

BRIARWOOD MASSACRE

SOUL SURVIVOR SPEAKS OUT

Once an esteemed treatment center, the name Briarwood Sanitorium has become synonymous with the medical atrocities that were discovered there late last week. The institution is now being referred to as a modern-day "Bedlam" with patients found to be subjected to neglect, abuse, and systemic torture. The horrors of Briarwood were brought to light by Dr. Adrian Lambert, a physician and advocate for holistic care as well as the only surviving employee, after the murder of his colleagues drew his attention to the facility's basement, where patients were found locked in cages and chained to the walls.

WHAT REALLY HAPPENED TO THE EMPLOYEES OF LOCAL SANITORIUM?

"Basement of Horrors"

It's unclear who initiated the massacre of the sanitorium's long-term staff while some claim the vigilante-style justice was warranted. Briarwood first opened its doors as a tuberculosis treatment center before transitioning to general patient care. Its residents, which include children and adults with intellectual disabilities, show signs of physical and sexual abuse, medical incompetence, and neglect. Many deaths occurred under suspicious circumstances, and a mass grave containing skeletal remains was discovered on the grounds, along with individual gravesites marked by wooden crosses.

The facility's closure followed a federal judge's order, strengthened by Dr. Lambert's detailed report of the ethics violations he witnessed firsthand under the employ of Dr. Hare and Dr. Burke (now deceased). These cases underscore a grim history of abuse and neglect in mental health institutions worldwide. While many of these facilities have been closed or reformed, the legacy of their atrocities continues to impact survivors and their communities. Acknowledging these dark chapters is crucial in preventing such abuses in the future and ensuring that mental health care prioritizes the dignity and rights of all individuals.

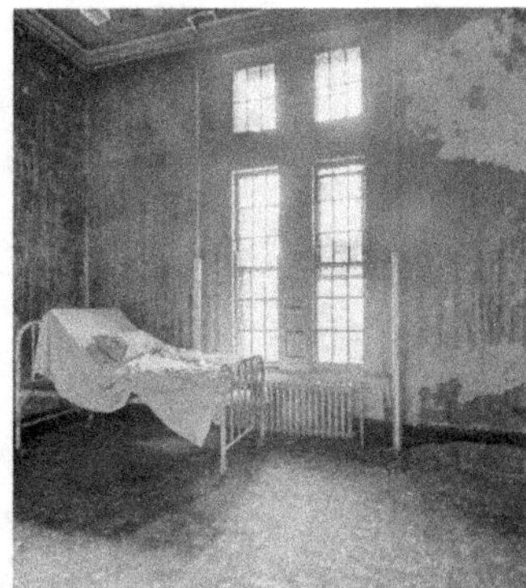

Patients found in cages and chained to walls and metal beds.

FROM THE AUTHOR:

Please note that the author does not in any way condone the behavior portrayed in this book. The main character's traumatic background was not described to excuse his actions but to show that people are more than one dimensional. That you can be both victim and perpetrator, and that one does not cancel out the other. You as a reader, as a person, can feel sorry for the child that someone was and still hate the adult they became.

ACKNOWLEDGMENTS

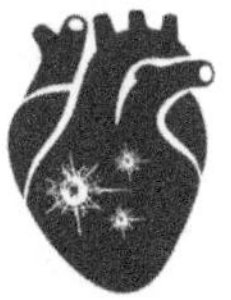

Thanks to everyone who has been a part of this long-ass process. To everyone who has shared, liked, commented, and preordered. To those of you who took a chance on me and my fucked-up brain. And to those who love the fictional characters that live rent free in my head. I could not have done it without you, and I am so very humbled.

I also wanted to say thank you to my ARC readers, who are taking time out of their busy schedules to read and review my book. And thank you to those of you who went as far as to read and review my prior publications too—"I see you" and I am so grateful for you.

A special thanks to Dahlia Reign (as always) for beta reading.

ALSO BY SYBIL KNIGHT

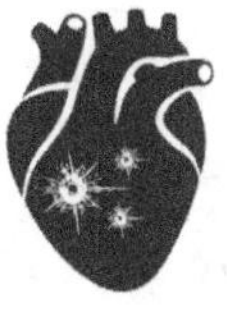

THE TRUTH AND LIES DUET:

The Harsher the Truth

The Sweeter the Lies

THE RENEGADES SERIES:

Skin

Lamb

Bells

STANDALONE NOVELS:

Half Cocked

Kill Joy

STANDALONE NOVELLAS:

THE SINS OF OUR FATHERS

V CARD

I'LL BE SEEING YOU

THE MORE THE MERRIER

EAT YOUR HEART OUT

NUTCRACKER

MORE TITLES TO COME...

ABOUT THE AUTHOR

Sybil is a true east coaster with a love for true crime and caffeine. When she isn't working or writing, she is talking about working or writing.

Her stories range from gray to black, with darker themes throughout. She prefers heroines with a kick-ass mentality and the heroes who know how to rein them in. The mental and medical aspects of her books are well-researched, though they are given a humanistic approach and diagnoses aren't the focal points. She believes her characters don't need to wear labels in order to get their messages across.

Her books are mostly standalones, though her characters may interact and intersect worlds. Additionally, she works closely with and writes alongside author Dahlia Reign and some characters will appear in cameos in each of their publications.

SYBIL WELCOMES EMAILS FROM READERS IF THERE ARE CONCERNS OR QUESTIONS REGARDING ANY OF HER PUBLICATIONS.

EMAIL: AUTHORSYBILKNIGHT@GMAIL.COM

www.ingramcontent.com/pod-product-compliance
Lightning Source LLC
Chambersburg PA
CBHW060448300726
48975CB00008B/2433